No Vacation from Murder

Switching on the light she fumbled for the receiver, her mind running ahead. . . . To her astonishment, the caller was Eddy Horner.

'Sorry to ring you at this hour, Mrs Makepeace,' he said, sounding worried. 'The fact is we're a bit bothered up here. Was young Wendy Shaw down at your place this evening?'

'I don't think so,' Marcia replied, trying to collect her wits. 'She wasn't at dinner, I'm quite sure of that. She could have been in the film show that followed—the hall was dark, of course, but I didn't see her coming out afterwards. Has—'

'We left her here in charge of the baby, at about seven. I drove my daughter up to Stoneham for a bit of dinner before we met her husband's train. The train was late, so we phoned Wendy, but there was no answer. We thought she must've gone to bed early, but whcn we got back twenty minutes ago, she wasn't here, and her coat and handbag have gone from her room.'

Marcia exclaimed, glancing at the clock which registered five minutes to twelve.

'I should never have thought she was the sort of girl to go off and leave a young baby alone like that.'

'She isn't,' Eddy Horner replied tersely. 'That's what's biting us. Sorry to have bothered you.'

D0048443

Other titles in the Walker British Mystery Series

ELIZABETH LEMARCHAND

No Vacation From Murder

WALKER AND COMPANY · NEW YORK

To C.M.L.

First published in the United States of America in 1974 by the
Walker Publishing Company, Inc.

This paperback edition first published in 1984.

Originally published in Great Britain under the title of *Let or
Hindrance*.

ISBN: 0-8027-3061-2

Library of Congress Catalog Card Number: 73-90727

Printed in the United States of America

10   9   8   7   6   5   4   3   2   1

Chief Characters

Horner's Holidays Ltd

Eddy Horner	Founder and owner of the firm
Michael Jay	Employees of the firm
Paul and Janice King	
Susan Crump	
Geoffrey Boothby	
Penny Townsend	Eddy Horner's married daughter
Wendy Shaw	Distant connection of the Horner family

St Julitta's School, Kittitoe

Philip Cary	Chairman of the Governors
Isabel Dennis	Governors
Donald Glover	
Hugh Stubbs	
Andrew Medlicott	Bursar
Marcia Makepeace	Domestic Bursar

Police

Constable Pike	Glintshire Constabulary
Detective-Superintendent Pollard and Detective-Sergeant Toye	New Scotland Yard

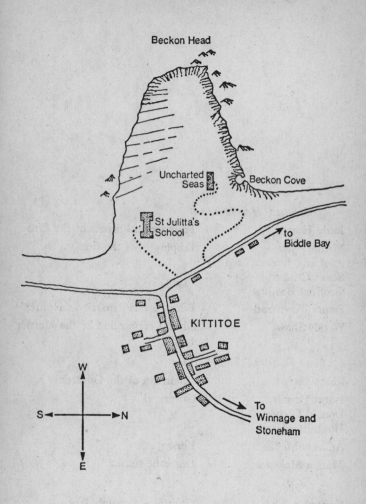

1

With full assent they vote.
Paradise Lost. Book Two

'Those in favour?'

From the Chair Philip Cary ran a practised eye round the library table.

'Those against?' he enquired perfunctorily. 'Right. We accept Endacott's estimate for the renewal of guttering and downpipes. On to Item Eight, then. Summer letting. Over to you, Bursar.'

He sat back, intercepting an amused glance from Miss Isabel Dennis, one of the governors in the know. There would be opposition, of course. Hugh Stubbs, founder of the Kittitoe Residents' Association, for one. Probably Lady Longridge, the Old Girls' representative...

The governors of St Julitta's School variously ticked their agendas, glanced at their watches, and looked hopefully in the direction of cups and saucers set out on a table. Professor Tyson, who had taken a lucky dip from the bookshelf behind him, continued to read a life of Bismarck, balancing the volume discreetly on his knee.

Andrew Medlicott, the school bursar, cleared his throat nervously and took up some correspondence neatly clipped together.

'I have to report, sir, that the Committee of the Frensham Children's Home has accepted the increased rental we agreed on at our last meeting. I have here a letter from the

1

Secretary booking our premises for the third and fourth weeks in July, as usual.'

There was a murmur of satisfaction, but Mrs Withers, a brisk hatted woman in tweeds, sniffed audibly.

'Of course they've accepted. They're not fools. Where else would they get amenities like ours at such ridiculously low cost? In my opinion, our parents are subsidizing them heavily.'

'The gross rental received is surely not the only aspect of the situation?' came Hugh Stubbs' thin dry voice. 'Up to the present the Frensham people have at least shown a responsible attitude towards our property, and refrained from making public nuisances of themselves.'

He looked pointedly across the table through his rimless spectacles at Donald Glover, who had developed a caravan site on the edge of the village.

'I'm sure we all agree that the new arrangement with Frensham is most satisfactory,' the Chairman interposed. 'They've certainly been model tenants up to now. Carry on, Bursar.'

Andrew Medlicott exchanged the Frensham correspondence for a sheet of notes.

'This year we have had an application for a let for the second and third weeks of August,' he announced. 'It is from Mr Horner of Uncharted Seas, and he is offering exactly double the rent Frensham is paying.'

The languishing meeting was galvanized by this information.

'One moment, ladies and gentlemen,' Philip Cary broke in, raising his voice above the buzz of conversation. 'Let's hear the facts first, shall we?'

'Mr Horner,' Andrew Medlicott resumed, 'has, of course, been obliged to cancel all Horner Holidays based on his hotel at Biddle Bay, as a result of the fire there. However, he is most anxious that the Horner Discovery Fortnight held in this area shall go ahead if possible, and has applied to rent the school for this purpose.'

Hugh Stubbs, who had been opening and shutting his mouth like a goldfish in a bowl, was the first to get the floor.

'It's a gross impertinence,' he stuttered. 'Expecting us to open the place to any Tom, Dick and Harry who can pay

2

what he charges. They could be highly undesirable—hippies, drug addicts…'

Donald Glover, a stocky man with a knowing eye, squared himself for action.

'The last speaker's talking through his hat,' he cut in brusquely. 'Why, these Discovery Fortnights as Eddy Horner calls them are highbrow stuff—lectures on seaweed and old houses and what-have-you. They only attract serious types. Retired people, a lot of 'em, looking for something to fill up their time. We'd be a pack of fools to turn down a good offer like this.'

Philip Cary allowed the wrangling to take its course. Hugh Stubbs continued to expostulate angrily. Lady Longridge wondered if letting to Horner's Holidays mightn't cheapen St Julitta's just a little? One had to think of the parents. An orphanage was rather different, surely? Canon Arthur Fuller, vicar of the parish of Kittitoe, was in favour of encouraging people's instructive hobbies, and at the same time of benefiting the school's finances. Donald Glover continued to back the Horner application with ham-fisted enthusiasm, thereby developing sales resistance among the undecided.

Isabel Dennis looked at him thoughtfully, wondering what lay behind his attitude. A prosperous local business man and a former St Julitta parent, his election to the school's governing body had eventually become inevitable, but so far the latter had failed to assimilate him. She decided on a diversion.

'Mr Chairman,' she asked, 'if we decide to let to Mr Horner, what would happen about domestic arrangements? Frensham bring their own staff, don't they?'

'I'm glad you've raised this point,' Philip Cary replied. 'Perhaps Miss Prince will come in on it?'

He turned to the headmistress, up to now tactfully silent on his right. Mr Horner, it appeared, had called to see her on this matter. He had suggested that Mrs Makepeace, the domestic bursar, should be asked if she would give up part of her summer holiday to run the housekeeping side of the Discovery Fortnight. He had offered very generous terms, both to her, and to any members of her staff willing to take on a holiday job. After thinking it over, both Mrs Makepeace

3

and an adequate number of her helpers had accepted Mr Horner's offer.

'Now that there's a question of this second let,' Miss Prince went on, 'I feel rather bad about my Canadian trip. I don't know whether after all—'

'Put any ideas of that sort right out of your head,' the Chairman told her, amid a chorus of agreement. 'Go off and have the holiday of a lifetime, as the travel agents' blurbs say. Mr Medlicott and Mrs Makepeace can perfectly well hold the fort, and come to that, Mr Horner himself is within shouting distance.'

Donald Glover remarked that Marcia Makepeace was a grand girl, bang on top of her job, and the pair of them would be a match for anybody.

Ignoring him, Mrs Withers asked if the Discovery Fortnight would have some responsible Horner staff in charge of its activities.

Certainly, Philip Cary told her. A Mr Michael Jay would be in overall charge, who had run Fortnights at Biddle Bay for the past few years, and there would be three other lecturers and a hostess, the wife of one of them.

Seeing that the steam was running out of the discussion, and that the ayes were going to have it, he invited a proposition from the meeting. Successfully avoiding Donald Glover's eye, he accepted one from Canon Fuller, to the effect that the school should be let to Mr Horner for the second and third weeks in August, subject to a satisfactory legal agreement. Professor Tyson surfaced smartly from the Franco-Prussian War, and seconded. Hugh Stubbs and Lady Longridge chose abstention in preference to certain defeat.

'Those in favour?' Philip Cary asked. 'Thank you. Those against?...I declare the motion carried. On to Item Nine, then. Any other business?'

At the beginning of the Second World War St Julitta's had been evacuated from the south coast to the less vulnerable village of Kittitoe on the west coast, where it established itself in the Headland Hotel. This was an elongated building on a terrace at the landward end of Beckon Head, a spectacular mass of rock rearing up out of the Atlantic. The terrace

4

ended seaward in low cliffs overlooking the beach. There was a south aspect, and a stupendous view along the coast. Parents acclaimed the health-giving ozone, the facilities for sea-bathing and riding, and the aesthetic quality of the new location. When the war ended, St Julitta's remained at Kittitoe. Gradually, as building restrictions were relaxed, the hotel was expanded, and made more suitable for its new function. In a comparatively short space of time the school became integrated into the neighbourhood.

Philip Cary was the last of the governors to leave the meeting at which the summer holiday lets were agreed upon. Soon after five he was going down the drive in his car. Emerging on to the road he turned left, and immediately left again, into the drive of Uncharted Seas, the home of Eddy Horner, founder and owner of Horner's Holidays, a well-known travel agency.

It had been a perfect early spring day, and after gaining height he drew up to enjoy the panorama of sunset sky and darkening sea. Ahead of him rose the massive black silhouette of Beckon Head. The lights of Kittitoe were reflected in the driving mirror, and far away to the south the beam from a lighthouse swept rhythmically over the water. The excrescence of Donald Glover's caravan site was happily swallowed up in the dusk.

Uncharted Seas was a large bungalow, built by Eddy Horner regardless of cost. It was not immediately above St Julitta's, but slightly further out towards the headland. An elongated building like the school, it was strung out along a similar terrace at a higher level. Behind it a path led up another fifty feet to a notch in the spine of the promontory. On the far side of this a flight of steps provided the only land access to Beckon Cove, an enchanting small cove fringed with shingle and sand at low tide. Before going into Uncharted Seas Philip Cary went up the path, and stood looking down into the Cove whose gently rising and falling waters mirrored the golden afterglow of sunset.

Eddy Horner came to the front door to let him in.

'Haven't I told you to walk right in?' he demanded. 'Nice of you to come up,' he added, leading the way to the long south-facing sitting room overlooking the sea.

5

'It's all yours,' Philip Cary told him, with a gesture in the direction of the school. 'Second and third weeks of August. You'll be getting it officially from Medlicott.'

Eddy Horner's wide mouth upturned at the corners expanded into a grin, and he gave a satisfied chortle. A balding little man in a fisherman's jersey, he suggested a friendly but sagacious kobbold.

'Thought my offer would fetch you lot down there,' he said. 'Whisky?'

'Thanks, I will.'

A log fire was burning on the hearth. Philip Cary subsided gratefully into an armchair, and contemplated the affluent comfort of the room. It's got a bit bleak without Penny's feminine touches, though, he thought. Eddy Horner, twice a widower, had only one child, a daughter by his second marriage. In the previous summer she had married Bob Townsend, a promising young Horner executive, now being trained up for his father-in-law's shoes.

The clinking of glasses heralded Eddy's return from the extensive bar at the far end of the room.

'Daresay you think I'm a bloody old fool,' he said, setting down a drinks tray, 'but the Horner Discovery Fortnights mean a lot to me. What we make out of 'em's chicken feed, but it's knowing that they show a few folk that there's more to life than bingo and the box. You'd be surprised at the letters we get. Say when.'

'When. You're a romantic, of course, Eddy,' Philip said, taking the glass held out to him. 'And by way of being a philanthropist. Cheers.'

'Cheers. That I'm not. I've made a packet out of Horner's Holidays. Mind you, I've always given value for money. No misleading ads, and that goes for long before the Trade Descriptions Act.'

They sipped their drinks in companionable silence.

'Talking of making a packet, how's Bob doing?' Philip enquired presently.

'Pretty well. Got imagination, and his head screwed on into the bargain. And he knows what work is. Tourism's booming, of course. Seen how the shares are keeping up?'

6

'I have. Wish I had a few more myself. What's the news of Penny?'

'Fine. She rang yesterday, after her check-up. The doctor says everything's OK.'

'June, isn't it?'

'End of the first week. She'll be down here with the baby by the end of the month, and stay for the summer. Bob can't leave the office in the height of the season, of course, but he'll run down weekends. Then he and Penny'll go off on their own in October, leaving the kid and its nurse here till they get back.'

'You can thank your lucky stars you've got a separate guest wing,' Philip said with feeling. 'Margaret and I are flat out after relays of grandchildren in the summer holidays. Which reminds me, she wants to know when you're coming over for a meal?'

When this point had been settled, he heaved himself up out of his chair and took his departure, Eddy Horner standing at the front door with hand raised in a friendly salute as he drove off.

Glad the let went through for the old boy, he thought, heading for his home in a neighbouring village. That damn fool Glover nearly stymied the whole thing, throwing his weight about like that. Wonder why he was so keen on Horner having the place? They're both in the local tourist market.

2

Bottom. Are we all met?
Quince. Pat, pat; and here's a marvellous
         convenient place for our rehearsal.
         A Midsummer Night's Dream.

Act 3 Scene i

On the afternoon of Thursday, August 5th, Marcia
Makepeace returned to Kittitoe to make her final preparations for the Horner Discovery Fortnight, due to start on the
following Saturday.

The drive of St Julitta's was deserted, and the school's
long façade had the blank look of an institution out of action.
Getting out of her car she unlocked the front door, and
walked into the airless silence of the entrance hall. As she did
so footsteps came hurrying from the direction of the kitchen
quarters. Mrs Bond, the gardener's wife, appeared, plump
and cheerful in a cotton frock with a pattern of sunflowers.

'There now, I said to George there's Mrs Makepeace's
car,' she exclaimed triumphantly. 'Glad to see you back,
dear. Have you had a nice holiday?'

'Fine, thanks, Mrs Bond,' Marcia told her. 'I've been staying with my sister and her family on their farm in Sussex.'

'That's right.' Mrs Bond shot a quick glance at her.
'Everything been all right here for you and George?'

During the holidays the Bonds moved into the school
from the gardener's cottage to act as caretakers. As she
listened to a breathless account of the Frensham let and other
matters, Marcia gathered that there was no domestic crisis
needing her immediate attention.

'And before I forgets it,' Mrs Bond broke off from her
narrative to say, 'Mrs Medlicott looked in with a note for you

this morning, and they're expecting you round to supper. But there's a couple of nice lamb chops in the fridge if you don't feel like going out again.'

'I think I'll go,' Marcia said. 'It'll save time in the morning if I see Mr Medlicott about one or two things tonight.'

'Right you are then, dear. I've got your tea all ready on a tray, and I'll send it up in the service lift straight away.'

She hurried off purposefully. Marcia collected her belongings from the car, and went upstairs to her rooms on the second floor. There was a pile of correspondence on the table in her sitting room. As she looked quickly through it for any personal letters she remembered with a stab that there was now no one in the world whose letters really mattered to her. Before her husband had been killed in the car crash two years ago, she'd lived for the sight of his sprawling hand-writing during his brief absences from home.

She glanced round the room. There were flowers to welcome her: Mrs Bond had even put a vase of roses by Stephen's photograph. People at St Julitta's were so kind, like the Medlicotts remembering to ask her to supper this evening. Still, she'd have to move on to something a bit more challenging soon, or she'd begin to vegetate.

Over her tea she slit open the manila envelopes of school correspondence and sorted their contents into little heaps. Then she went downstairs to check that the stores ordered in for the Discovery Fortnight had arrived. She became involved with both the Bonds, and it was later than she had realized when she managed to break away and bath and change before going out.

Ready to start, she paused for a moment before a long mirror to scrutinize her hemline. Tall, slender and loose-knit, she moved this way and that with an easy grace. The blue-grey of the frock matched her eyes, and set off her golden-brown hair. As she considered, her teeth nipped the lower lip of her rather wide mouth.

It was a bit short, she decided. Skirts were definitely dropping. Snatching up her handbag she hurried down to her car. A high tide was sweeping up the beach. An intermittent hiccuping came from the blowhole, an air shaft leading from a cave in the cliffs below to an opening in the school grounds. Inevitably named Sir Toby Belch, it was the pride of St Julitta's. The sun was dropping towards Beckon Head, and the sea darkening to turquoise. It's a marvellous spot, she thought, getting into the car. One even feels happy here in patches.

The Medlicotts had a bungalow on the outskirts of Kittitoe. Andrew came out to greet her, and in the warmth of his welcome Marcia recognized the usual tinge of relief at the arrival of support. He would never quite recover from the trauma of finding himself an unemployed senior executive in his early fifties. The modest bursarship at St Julitta's had been his lifeline back to self-respect, and in gratitude he slaved and fussed unnecessarily over the school's business. As they went into the bungalow, Marcia heard that Frensham had blotted its copybook by cracking a wash-basin, but had paid up without demur.

'Fine,' she said, deliberately breezy, 'a brand new one for free... This is most awfully good of you, Daphne,' she added, as her hostess emerged from the kitchen.

Daphne Medlicott was small, brown and warmhearted. She kissed Marcia affectionately.

'Lovely that you're back,' she said. 'Everything's in the oven, so we can sit over drinks and hear what you've been doing.'

It was a pleasantly relaxed evening, and it was not until the coffee cups were empty that Andrew was allowed to produce a series of lists for Marcia.

'Horner's have kept the numbers down to eighty,' he told her. 'That's two coachloads for expeditions if everyone goes. The five lecturers are bringing cars.'

They discussed the possibility of keeping one of the bedroom wings closed, to cut down on cleaning.

'Two of the lecturers—a Mr and Mrs King—are coming in some species of dormobile, and like to sleep in it to get away from it all,' Andrew said, consulting a letter.

'I don't blame them. I often wish I were non-resident myself,' Marcia remarked. 'Wait a bit. This may just do the trick, if we can fit the other three into the sick bay. Who are they?'

'Michael Jay—you met him, of course, when he came down

in the spring term to discuss details. Miss Susan Crump, and Mr Geoffrey Boothby.'

'Well, let's hope Miss Susan Crump won't feel her virtue's at risk if we put her in the sick bay with a couple of males,' Marcia said, making notes. 'Parking's going to be a problem. How many of the eighty are bringing their own cars?'

They went into this and other matters at some length.

'I only hope there won't be an outsize hitch of some sort,' Andrew Medlicott said, as she finally rose to go.

'Why on earth should there be?' Marcia replied bracingly. 'After all, if one of the Fortnight people turns out to be a murderer or something, it's not our responsibility, is it?'

On Friday morning St Julitta's presented a scene of intensive domestic activity. Workmanlike in a white overall, Marcia Makepeace supervised the combined operation in progress while attending to a number of miscellaneous matters. As she was arranging flowers she was called to the telephone.

'The domestic bursar speaking,' she said.

'Well, well, well,' came a hearty masculine voice. 'So our Mrs Makepeace is back on the job. That's great. Don Glover here. How's it going, my dear?'

'Perfectly well, thank you,' she replied coolly.

'All lined up for Operation Horner, eh? Fine, fine. This show's got to go like a bomb, hasn't it? It could be quite a thing for St J's, y'know. Eddy Horner's a pal of mine. Get him even more interested in the school, and you don't know what mightn't come out of it. Matter of fact I put him on to the idea of renting the place.'

'I really can't see any reason why everything shouldn't run smoothly, Mr Glover.'

'Sure, sure, with you doing the running, my dear—ha! ha! I told Eddy we'd got a winner in you. Just give me a tinkle if you want a bit of help. Goodbye for now, then.'

He rang off.

My God, that man, Marcia thought briefly as she went back to her flowers.

Later in the morning she was wanted on the telephone again. To her surprise the caller was Mr Horner. He was pleasant and to the point. Would she kindly tell the Fort-

11

night staff when they turned up that he'd be pleased to see them for drinks after dinner that evening. Say nine o'clock, at Uncharted Seas. And he hoped she would join the party. Mr and Mrs Medlicott were coming along.

She had always felt curious about the bungalow and its inmates, and accepted at once.

'I'll look forward to seeing you up here then,' he said. 'And thank you once again, Mrs Makepeace, for taking on this job for me in your holidays.'

Before she could reciprocate with thanks for his generous terms, he rang off.

Marcia had the self-assurance of the professionally competent. As she waited for the Horner staff to arrive in the early evening, she was surprised to find herself feeling quite apprehensive. What was her status going to be during the Fortnight? Responsibility without authority was always difficult. She began to wish that someone would arrive and start things moving.

In the event three cars drew up within minutes of each other. Watching from the front door she saw Michael Jay emerge from the first. He came up the steps, a tall, dark and rather solidly built man of about forty, with the air of good-humoured capability which she remembered from their earlier meeting, and which she now found reassuring. He greeted her warmly, and turned to introduce the couple who had got out of the dormobile. Paul King was a younger, sandy-haired man with a lively face and hornrims, and his wife Janice a small with-it platinum blonde. The occupant of the battered estate car which had brought up the procession was a stocky woman of about fifty, already garbed and shod for energetic outdoor activities.

'Meet Susan Crump, our biologist,' Michael Jay said. 'There's one more of us to come, Geoff Boothby. He'll be along any time now—he only lives over at Winnage.'

'I've laid on dinner for seven o'clock, Mr Jay,' Marcia told him. 'I hope that suits everybody? And there's an invitation from Mr Horner, to go up to his bungalow for drinks at nine.'

'That all sounds jolly good. Well, if you'll just show us the lie of the land, Mrs Makepeace, we'd better make a start on humping our gear in. There's quite a bit of it, I'm afraid.'

A mountain of boxes, bags, rolls of maps and suitcases rapidly built up on the immaculate floor of the entrance hall. Seeing Marcia looking at it ruefully, Paul King grinned as he staggered in with a ciné projector.

'Not to worry,' he assured her. 'We'll soon clear this little lot. That must be Geoff arriving.'

A roar and a screech of brakes came from the drive, and a few moments later a long-haired young man in jeans and a faded shirt appeared, a scowl on his face. Intelligent, but hopelessly shy, Marcia diagnosed, as he mumbled something in reply to her greeting. She was feeling cheerful and interested. It all looked like being much easier and more friendly than she had expected, and there was loud approval of St Julitta's amenities.

'This is just fabulous,' Janice King said, as her husband parked the dormobile on a site behind the school buildings indicated by Marcia. 'Paul, Mrs Makepeace says there's a bathroom and loo just up the stairs inside this door.'

'Super,' he agreed. 'You know it's sheer heaven to clear off and have a spot of peace at the end of the day.'

'The rest of us are doing nicely, too,' Michael Jay remarked, strolling up and joining them. 'We're segregated in the sick bay. Really imaginative of you, that, Mrs Makepeace. Of course, you'll be having dinner with us tonight, won't you?'

Marcia was pleased.

'I'd like to very much,' she said. 'In the ordinary way, of course, I'll have to be behind the scenes.'

She had taken special pains over this first meal, and it was highly successful. In the course of it she learnt who did what during the Fortnight. In addition to having overall responsibility, Michael Jay lectured on local settlement and buildings of historic and architectural interest.

'From the Iron Age camp on Biddle Down onwards,' he told her. 'Geoff does the natural landscape and local geology, and takes enthusiasts fossil hunting. Susan's line is plant life, and the things you find in rock pools and along the beach. Paul's our bird man—a very popular line, that, and our photographic expert into the bargain. He films the expeditions and whatever as we go along, and shows the finished product on the last evening, when it's always a smash hit. Janice has the diciest job as hostess. She has to be a walking information bureau, first aid post, smoother-out of grievances, organizer of evening do's—the lot.'

Janice King, looking with-it in scarlet trousers and white silk top, agreed that hostessing could be bloody at times.

'The crowd you get varies a lot,' she said. 'Usually they're very decent types, but it's extraordinary how one or two grumblers can get the whole lot disgruntled. Let's hope we'll be lucky this time, that's all, and get good weather. Are we allowed to smoke in here, Mrs Makepeace?' she asked Marcia, pausing in the act of reaching for her handbag.

'Of course. What do you do about smoking in the dining room when everyone's here, Mr Jay?'

'Michael, please. We ask them to refrain until the coffee stage. This really is coffee, if I may say so.'

'Remember the muck that passed for coffee at Biddle?' Geoff Boothby asked unexpectedly, then going pink with embarrassment.

'Served at the end of what they called the evening meal,' Michael Jay replied. 'A loathsome expression. You can't think what a difference it makes to have it called dinner, Mrs Makepeace, quite apart from the sort of food you've given us tonight.'

'Marcia, please. I hope we can keep it up, that's all. However hard you try, food cooked in bulk never turns out quite the same.'

'If it only turns out half as good as this, we shall be doing nicely, thank you,' Paul King assured her. 'Do we walk up to the Old Man's place, or take the cars?'

'Not Geoff's car, for heaven's sake,' said Susan Crump emphatically. 'It'd wake the dead, let alone the precious Horner grandchild.'

'Here!' protested its owner indignantly.

In the end they all packed into Michael Jay's Hillman, and Susan Crump's estate car, and drove up to Uncharted Seas in lighthearted mood.

All the Horner staff appeared to know Eddy, who radiated bonhomie as he received congratulations on his new status as grandfather. His daughter, Penny Townsend, was an attractive young woman, clearly exhilarated at having produced a son and heir. The women of the party were swept off to admire Edward Robert Horner Townsend, asleep in a cot in his mother's bedroom.

'Plain hideous, isn't he?' remarked Penny dotingly. 'So not to worry about saying who he's like. Anyone care to see round the bungalow before I clock in for the ten pm feed?'

The architect had certainly done a first class job on a difficult site, Marcia reflected. No doubt he'd been given carte blanche. The self-contained guest wing with its kitchenette might have been designed for visiting grandchildren. She surveyed the kitchen proper with a critical eye, and could not fault its planning or equipment. Returning to the sitting room, they were led out on to the terrace. An enormous full moon was riding in a cloudless sky, its path scintillating on the water. Lingering behind the others, Marcia found Eddy Horner standing beside her.

'Takes a bit of beating, doesn't it?' he asked, with engaging pride.

'I don't think you could have possibly found a more wonderful site,' she told him. 'I expect you've travelled all over the world, and seen some marvellous places, though, haven't you?'

'I've been around a bit,' he admitted. 'Before we got so big I made it a rule to OK any place we sent a Horner holiday to. But there's the heck of a lot of the world I've never seen, and I'm getting an old chap now. That brat in there'll be vetting the moon for the firm before he's done. Here, you haven't had a drink yet.'

Inside there was a large assortment of drinks and snacks, and the atmosphere was becoming convivial. Even Andrew Medlicott, Marcia noticed, was almost animated as he discussed birdwatching with the Kings, and accepted an invitation to join an expedition to a remote raven colony down the coast. Canon Fuller and his wife had arrived, and appeared to have discovered some link with Susan Crump, which the three of them were discussing vigorously. Geoff Boothby had made contact with a rather stolid young girl who had been introduced as a relative of the Horners', come to lend a hand with the baby. The pair sat together on a small

15

sofa, saying little, but seemingly enjoying each other's company.

'All we want to round off this party's Bob,' Eddy Horner remarked from the hearth during a sudden lull in the conversation. 'Pity it's the one weekend he couldn't get down.'

'When does he get down as a rule?' Michael Jay asked.

'Friday nights. Penny and I run up to Stoneham, to meet him off the London train at just after ten. Hey, who's that at the door? Excuse me...'

He vanished into the hall. A couple of minutes later he returned with Don Glover.

'See who's here, folks,' he said as heads turned. 'Another of the school governors come to give Horner's the onceover. Mr Donald Glover.'

'That's not fair,' Don Glover protested, not displeased. 'How was I to know there was a party on? I just dropped in for a friendly chat with Mr Horner. What's mine? Well, I won't say no to a whisky and splash, thanks.'

Eddy Horner began on a round of introductions. Marcia noticed that Geoff Boothby had gone to the bar, and unobtrusively slipped into his place on the sofa. Marginally situated, she hoped to escape Don Glover's tiresome facetiousness.

Wendy Shaw improved on closer acquaintance. She was not in the least pretty by conventional standards, but her face showed character, and there was a pleasant unspoilt freshness about her. Marcia learnt that she was in training as a nursery nurse, and had one more year to go. Perhaps money was tight at home, for she seemed glad to have a holiday job. Asked if she liked Kittitoe, she became quite enthusiastic. It was a fabulous place and so was the bungalow. Uncle Eddy and Cousin Penny were so kind. They often took her for super car drives, and she was learning to surf. They wanted her to join the Youth Club as a holiday member, but she wasn't keen. You'd feel a bit out of it, not knowing anyone. The baby was sweet, and good as gold.

At this point Geoff Boothby returned with a glass in each hand. He was at a loss to find his seat occupied, and Marcia took pity on him, and extricated herself after a few friendly remarks. She joined Daphne Medlicott, and under

16

cover of the rising volume of conversation in the room they compared their reactions to the bungalow and the rest of the company.

Suddenly, as they were talking, it occurred to Marcia that it was odd that Don Glover had not been invited to the party, if, as he had told her, he had put Eddy Horner on to the idea of renting St Julitta's for the Fortnight. They could hardly be such tremendous buddies. And if they weren't, it was odd of Don Glover to gatecrash. He must have realized a party was on from the cars parked outside.

At this point her reflections were interrupted by the arrival of Paul King propelling a trolley laden with snacks.

3

But answer came there none—
Alice Through the Looking-Glass.
The Walrus and the Carpenter.

During the opening stages of the Discovery Fortnight
Marcia felt like a ghost visiting once familiar surroundings,
and finding them strangely altered and itself unrecognized.
Instead of the rhythmic ebb and flow of St Julitta's uniform
through the building, eccentrically dressed adults wandered
about at all hours, exchanging incomprehensible jargon such
as Hercynian folds, sociable plovers and the hairy-headed
hawkbit. To these she was an unidentified figure, either
ignored or given brief smiles of non-recognition. The Horner
staff were immersed in their own spheres. From time to
time Janice King contacted her on some domestic matter,
and was always friendly and appreciative, but apart from
this she found herself in an unaccustomed and depressing
isolation.

Fortunately there was plenty to occupy her. The com-
plimentary remarks about her catering had put her on her
mettle. The daily women were appalled by the mud and
messy specimens brought in, and needed jollying along and
frequent reminders of inflated pay packets to come. At intervals she studied the various programmes of lectures, dis-
cussions and expeditions on the noticeboard in the entrance
hall, but no suggestion was made that she might care to take
part in any of them.

On the first Tuesday evening she supervised the serving
of dinner, had her own on a tray in her office, and then re-

tired upstairs to the solitude of her sitting room. She was tidying her desk preparatory to relaxing when there was a knock at the door.

'Come in,' she called, expecting to see one of the kitchen staff with some query about the following day.

The door opened tentatively, and Michael Jay's head came round it.

'Is this absolutely not on,' he asked, 'invading your private territory?'

'Of course it's on,' she replied genuinely pleased at the prospect of a human contact. 'Do come in, Mr Jay. Nothing's badly unstuck, I hope?'

He stared at her in blank amazement as he sat down.

'Good God, no! I just felt I must track you down to say how simply fine it all is. The old hands are saying that we've never been so comfortable on a Fortnight, or had such super meals.'

'How nice of you to come and tell me,' she replied, feeling a small glow of pleasure. 'I'll pass it on to my staff. Would you care for another cup of coffee? I was just going to make myself some.'

'Lovely,' he said. 'My coffee potential's unlimited.'

Returning presently with a tray she sensed that her sitting room had been scrutinized with interest.

'Do smoke,' she invited.

'Really? I'm a pipe-smoker, as you may have noticed.'

'It smells much nicer than cigarette smoke. Black or white?'

As she poured the coffee, she was aware that she had noticed. In fact, now that he was sitting opposite her, she realized how much she had registered about Michael Jay. That he smiled with his eyes as well as his lips, for instance, and that his way of speaking was considered, but not a bit pompous.

Conversation was easy, if general. She gathered that the Fortnight was off to a good start. It seemed to be a keen crowd, and there were no signs of any friction as yet, in spite of one or two compulsive talkers. Kittitoe was a much better base than Biddle Bay. As Michael Jay enlarged on this,

Marcia began to feel that she knew very little of the neighbourhood.

'You know, I've been here for eighteen months,' she told him, 'but you're making me feel that I've been pretty unenterprising about going places.'

'Well, here's your chance.' He smiled at her, and extracted a copy of the Fortnight programme from his pocket. 'You needn't tell me that anybody as competent as you are needs to be on the job the whole time. Drop in on any of the lectures you like the sound of, and come on one or two expeditions. What about Thursday's, for instance, to the Saxon village that's being excavated over at Ingatshoe? It's fascinating. Perhaps you've seen it already?'

'No, I haven't,' she said, realizing that he would be taking it himself, and becoming suddenly hesitant.

If Michael Jay noticed a change in her manner, he gave no sign of it.

'Jolly good,' he said, 'That's settled. I'm conducting the trip, but there's positively no obligation to trail along and listen, if you'd rather wander round on your own. And now I suppose it's my duty to go and mingle below. Thanks so much for the coffee.'

When he had gone Marcia sat motionless for some time. Stephen...she thought, staring at the photograph on her desk. Only a few days ago she'd felt that awful pang about his letters, here in this room. Yet, in the short space of time since, she'd developed this extraordinary awareness of another man whom she hardly knew...Too honest with herself not to face the fact, she experienced an almost intolerable tension. Then her pride and a spark of self-mockery resolved the situation. Really, it was quite preposterous to read a reciprocal awareness on Michael Jay's part into an invitation to visit an archaeological dig...

She got up abruptly, and bore off the coffee tray to the pantry, deciding at the same time to take the sensible step of joining in some of the Fortnight's activities. It would give her mind something to bite on, anyway.

This decision proved rewarding. New interests were suggested to her, and she came to know the Horner staff better. Paul King, as she had been led to expect, was much in evidence. The lectures she went to were all illustrated by his superb colour slides, and his birdwatching expeditions were always heavily oversubscribed. She found him amusing and generally very good company, although intolerant of the slightest disruption of his plans by those of his colleagues. Janice was a hard worker and most efficient, never ruffled by minor crises, and an excellent organizer of the Fortnight's social activities. An occasional waspish remark about her clientele made Marcia suspect a lack of human sympathy under her camaraderie. Susan Crump, however, improved on further acquaintance. Her brusque manner concealed great kindness, and she had a delightful dry humour. The dark horse of the team was undoubtedly Geoff Boothby. Usually tongue-tied in company, and decidedly sulky-looking, he developed the fluency of the enthusiast in the realms of his own interests, and showed a childlike excitement over Sir Toby Belch which Marcia found quite engaging. She was intrigued at seeing Wendy Shaw with him in his car one evening. Had Wendy unsuspected scintillating quality, too, she wondered?

Despite her efforts to do so she was unable to ignore the fact that she was drawn to Michael Jay, and humiliatingly aware of his presence or absence. As before, self-mockery seemed the most feasible line to take with herself, and it afforded her some relief from the tension which kept recurring at a deeper emotional level. She set off on the expedition to the Saxon village determined to behave towards him with easy detached friendliness. Seated beside him in the coach, however, it was impossible to keep the conversation on strictly impersonal lines throughout a forty mile drive. Her enquiries about the set-up at Horner's inevitably led on to his about St Julitta's and her work there. After a time she began to feel tiresomely conscious of her wedding ring, and suddenly angry that he might think that her marriage had broken up, she referred as casually as she could to Stephen's death. He was silent for a moment before making a conventionally sympathetic remark, but volunteered no information about any matrimonial relationship, past or present, of his own. As they neared home he suggested a drink at the King William, the Kittitoe pub, after dinner. She refused, on grounds of having things to see to for the following day, and then regretted it. A solitary and unhappy evening resulted, during which a deepening sense of disloyalty to Stephen alternated in her mind with the ache of the thought of Michael Jay's vanishing from her life at the end of the following week. Finally she went to bed feeling mentally and physically exhausted, slept heavily, and woke the next morning convinced that the best way to deal with a situation which had become intolerable was to avoid Michael as far as possible.

In this she met with little success. After breakfast she ran into him in a corridor.

'Well met,' he said, giving her a quick look. 'I was going to ask you if you could spare a few minutes to discuss arrangements for the last evening. I know it's a week away, but we usually have a mild sort of jamboree and I thought you might like to plan ahead. Perhaps I might drop in again this evening, and scrounge another cup of coffee?'

'By all means,' she said, in what she hoped was a normal voice. 'I'll expect you any time you're free after—say—half-past eight.'

As the day wore on she was exasperated with herself for feeling increasingly edgy, and when he arrived was at pains to greet him in a brisk and businesslike manner. He told her that there was a tradition of making the last evening of a Fortnight a bit festive. Perhaps there could be something just a bit special for dinner? Afterwards Paul King's film of all the activities was put on. People saw themselves in it, and it always went like a bomb. Then there was a small souvenir for everybody.

'Advertising, of course,' he said, 'but it goes down every time.'

'I can certainly put on a special dinner,' Marcia said. 'How about a few decorations in the dining room to brighten things up?'

'That would be super, if it doesn't mean an awful lot of extra work for you. By the way, we'll all be out to lunch that day. We've got a pretty good final expedition lined up —Starbury Bay. There's something for everybody over there.'

22

'Good,' Marcia replied. 'That'll give me a clear run to get things ready for the evening.'

A pause followed.

'When are you getting away yourself?' Michael Jay asked.

This was a switch to personal ground. She steadied her voice.

'I'm planning to stay on until the following Wednesday, to get everything in train for the beginning of term on the 9th. Then I needn't come back until the last minute.'

'Will you be in London during the week before that, by any chance?'

'I shall, as it happens,' she replied, contemplating her hands.

'Will you have dinner with me one evening, Marcia?'

Her world was dissolving and re-forming around her. After what seemed an eternity, she heard her voice, sounding a long way off, accepting the invitation. Then he was standing beside her, and very gently turning her face towards him. To her utter dismay she realized that her eyes were full of tears. Making a small gesture in the direction of Stephen's photograph, he stooped to kiss her.

'Not to worry, darling,' he said. 'Life has a way of working out, you know. We're not going to try to force the pace.'

He felt her relax in the curve of his arm, and they stayed still and silent. Suddenly distant strains of pop music were audible.

'Hell!' Michael exclaimed. 'I suppose I must go and join in idiotic antics, and play bridge with Senior Citizens. But I'm wangling time off during the weekend, come what may.'

He kissed her again, and was gone...

Retrospectively it always seemed to Marcia that from this point onward the Kittitoe Fortnight became a kind of non-time, unmeasurable by normal standards. In one sense it was all over at the drop of a hat, while in another aeons passed as she adapted herself to the incredible fact of a serenely developing relationship with Michael Jay. Then suddenly it was the last Friday morning, and she was handing out the last batch of picnic lunches.

Paul King took a packet for himself and another for Janice, and confided in her that he was hoping to engineer a slightly earlier return from the Starbury Bay expedition.

'I got some rather decent shots over at Winnage yesterday,' he said. 'I ought to have processed the film last night, but some of the crowd persuaded us to go along to the pub after dinner, and I didn't get it done until before breakfast this morning. That leaves all the editing for when we get back today.'

Marcia assured him that the sooner the party returned the better, as far as she was concerned. She wanted to get the buffet tea cleared away in good time, so that final preparations for the evening could go ahead.

After waving off the coaches she went back into the building, and settled down to the job of decorating the dining room.

At lunchtime she noticed that the sky had clouded over, and hoped that the weather would hold up until everyone got back, but by three o'clock a light drizzling rain had set in. Ten minutes later the telephone rang.

'Nothing dire, darling,' Michael Jay told her, 'but there's been some tiresome mix-up about the time for starting back. We're all getting wet—a lot of idiots haven't brought macs —and Paul's raising Cain because of editing the film he took yesterday.'

'Are you just starting back now?' she asked, looking at her watch.

'No, that's it. The drivers have vanished into thin air, leaving the coaches locked. The pubs are shut now, so it's pretty hopeless trying to track them down in a place like this.'

Marcia commiserated, and promised to have gallons of hot tea waiting.

'I'll go and break it to the kitchen staff,' she said. 'Thanks so much for ringing. Be seeing you soon, anyway.'

In fact it was nearly half-past five when the coaches drew up, and began to disgorge their wet and disgruntled passengers. Paul King, looking like thunder, pushed past and vanished in the direction of the laboratory. In reply to Marcia's question about sending him in some tea, Janice replied that he was in a filthy temper, and best left alone. Marcia accordingly concentrated on the general public, offering drying facilities and limitless cups of tea. The atmosphere

24

gradually became more cheerful. She was amused to see that Michael Jay was clearly put out by the contretemps. Wounded pride of a first-class organizer, she thought, recognizing a weakness of her own.

By dinner time public morale was restored, and when, punctually at seven o'clock, she flung wide the doors into the dining room, there were loud cries of approval. Christmas decorations borrowed from the school and clusters of balloons transformed the normally functional scene. There were vases of dahlias on the tables, piles of crackers, and the Horner souvenirs parcelled up in gay wrapping paper beside every plate. From behind the serving hatch she had the satisfaction of seeing her special four-course dinner go through without a hitch, and was just leaving the kitchen to have her own meal when she was startled by a concerted shout of 'we want Mrs Makepeace.'

Protest was useless and she was forcibly led into the dining room by a veteran Fortnighter, and presented with a colossal box of chocolates and a card bearing eighty-five signatures. Taken aback, and genuinely touched, she managed a brief speech of thanks which adroitly brought in her staff, and escaped to a final burst of clapping.

Later she slipped into the back of the assembly hall's gallery. By previous arrangement Michael was sitting just inside.

'All's well,' he told her. 'Paul's going to get the editing done, Janice says. We've kept them happy with one of his bird films.'

Not long afterwards this came to an end amid tumultuous applause, and the lights went up. A few minutes later Janice King appeared in front of the screen.

'Ladies and gentlemen,' she announced, 'Horner's Holidays presents the film of the year, the Discovery Fortnight at Kittitoe, 1971.'

There was more applause as the leader flashed on to the screen, turning to roars of laughter as the veteran Fortnighter of Marcia's presentation was seen emerging from his car on arrival, stern first.

The evening was undoubtedly being a roaring success, and a gregarious atmosphere persisted after the film show. A few stalwarts braved wind and rain for a farewell drink at the King William, but everyone else packed into the common rooms for refreshments and chat before going off to bed. It had been a busy day, and Marcia was glad to reach her own room at last. Tired but happy, she was being lulled to sleep by the noise of the wind and sea when her bedside telephone rang.

Switching on the light she fumbled for the receiver, her mind running ahead. Some family emergency of one of the Fortnighters? A good thing she had that bedroom list down in her office.

To her astonishment, the caller was Eddy Horner.

'Sorry to ring you at this hour, Mrs Makepeace,' he said, sounding worried. 'The fact is we're a bit bothered up here. Was young Wendy Shaw down at your place this evening?'

'I don't think so,' Marcia replied, trying to collect her wits. 'She wasn't at dinner, I'm quite sure of that. She could have been in the film show that followed—the hall was dark, of course, but I didn't see her coming out afterwards. Has—'

'We left her here in charge of the baby, at about seven. I drove my daughter up to Stoneham for a bit of dinner before we met her husband's train. The train was late, so we phoned Wendy, but there was no answer. We thought she must've gone to bed early, but when we got back twenty minutes ago, she wasn't here, and her coat and handbag have gone from her room.'

Marcia exclaimed, glancing at the clock which registered five minutes to twelve.

'I should never have thought she was the sort of girl to go off and leave a young baby alone like that.'

'She isn't,' Eddy Horner replied tersely. 'That's what's biting us. Sorry to have bothered you.'

Before Marcia could offer any help, he had rung off. She sank back on her pillows, feeling very disturbed. After a moment or two she realized why. Geoff Boothby had been one of those who had gone out after the film show.

4

Thou hadst a voice whose sound was like the sea...
Wordsworth. Sonnet.

From an early hour on the following morning St Julitta's resounded to the noise and confusion of eighty-five people preparing for departure. It was an unpropitious day of wind and rain, and Marcia could see signs of tempers wearing thin. In the intervals of keeping an eye on a running breakfast she emerged to lend a hand where she could.

It was a relief to catch sight of Geoff Boothby. He was more than usually dishevelled, and certainly looked tired. Could he and Wendy Shaw really have been fools enough to go off for a farewell run in the car, leaving the baby asleep, and had a breakdown or an accident? If so, they'd had it where Eddy Horner was concerned. Perhaps she was being unfair to Geoff, at any rate. At this point Marcia hurried to help an elderly lady who wanted to put through a telephone call to London, and for the moment stopped speculating on the matter.

By nine o'clock a considerable number of Fortnighters had already left by car, and the entrance hall was filling up with the luggage of those who were being taken by coach to catch trains at Stoneham. Marcia found herself overwhelmed by appreciative thanks for the comforts she had provided, and invitations to visit people when in their part of the country. Someone grabbed her arm, and she turned to encounter Susan Crump, enveloped in oilskins and a sou'wester.

'Fly, all is known,' Susan said with a grin. 'A bobby's asking for you. I've bunged him into your office.'

'Thanks awfully. I'd better go along.' Seized with unpleasant forebodings, Marcia hastily extricated herself.

Constable Pike, a familiar figure in Kittitoe with whom she had occasionally had minor dealings, rose to greet her as she came in. He had removed his helmet, and looked young and harassed.

'It's about the young lady who's missing from Mr Horner's place, Mrs Makepeace,' he told her. 'She still hasn't turned up. Mr Horner says he rang you last night, and asked if you'd seen her down here?'

Rightly interpreting this as a question, Marcia repeated the conversation as accurately as she could remember.

'Was the young lady in the habit of coming down here?' Constable Pike asked.

'I've never seen her here myself,' Marcia replied with perfect truth. 'We had a party last night to wind up the Discovery Fortnight which has been going on here, so perhaps Mr Horner thought someone had invited her to come along. But if she did, I didn't see her myself, and I was around nearly all the time.'

No, she thought, I'm under no obligation to say anything about her knowing Geoff Boothby. Not at this stage...not unless Michael thinks we ought to...

Constable Pike looked gloomy.

'It's a proper caper,' he said. 'Half the visitors on the move today, seeing it's Saturday, and most of 'em gone by now. Talk about making enquiries! And it's a hundred to one she's gone off with some chap, the way they are now. All very well Mr Horner saying she isn't that sort: they're all the same these days, girls are. Why, I wouldn't put it past your young ladies here, Mrs Makepeace, that I wouldn't.'

In spite of her anxious preoccupation Marcia laughed.

'Neither would I,' she agreed.

'Well, I'd better be going along and wasting somebody else's time,' he said, reaching for his helmet. 'I'm sorry to have troubled you, Mrs Makepeace, on a busy morning like this. Thank you for confirming that phone call.'

She showed him out by a side door, and returned to the scene just in time to see off the coach. Only a few people now remained, and the Horner staff had begun to load up the equipment they had brought for the Fortnight. She found herself being propelled towards her office by Michael Jay.

'What goes on?' he demanded. 'Susan said you'd been closeted with a bobby.'

'He came about Wendy Shaw. That girl who was helping Penny Townsend with the baby. She's disappeared. Eddy Horner rang me after I'd gone to bed last night, to ask if she'd been down here.'

'Good God! How awful for them. When did it happen?'

For the second time Marcia went into details of the telephone call. Michael eyed her shrewdly.

'What's biting you in all this?' he asked.

'You'll think I'm crazy, I expect,' she replied unwillingly, 'or a sensation-monger or something, but I can't help remembering that Geoff Boothby attached himself to her that evening we went up to Uncharted Seas, and I've seen her out in his car since, and he did go out after the film show last night.'

'True.' Michael frowned slightly. 'Come to think of it, I've seen them out in his car, and in the pub together. What time did Eddy ring you?'

'Five minutes to twelve.'

'I went up to bed about ten past. There was no light showing under his door or Susan's : I assumed they'd already turned in. I'm a light sleeper, too, and I'm pretty sure I'd have heard anyone coming in later. Anyhow, Geoff can't possibly have gone off with the girl, or he wouldn't be around this morning.'

'No, but do you think Wendy might have told him something about some other boy friend who was coming down to see her, or whatever? What I really mean is, ought I to have told Constable Pike that she and Geoff had been seeing something of each other?'

Michael took her hand and held it.

'No,' he said, 'I don't, darling. If Geoff had vanished into the blue as well, it would be a different kettle of fish. But as things are, it would start an unnecessary hare and be tough on Geoff. I think you're probably right about her having fixed for some chap to look her up at a time when she knew she'd be alone last night. Then he'd suggest a short run in his car, and they went off, had a breakdown, and she funked going back late to face Eddy and Penny Townsend. I expect she's making for home. If the police were taking it seriously, you know, they'd have been on the trail at first light instead of waiting until scores of people have pushed off. If you like, I'll just have a word with Geoff before he goes...Damn and blast all these people! Let's forget them, and concentrate on ourselves for a few minutes.'

A little later they returned to the entrance hall and ran into Janice King.

'Oh, there you are,' she said. 'Geoff couldn't find either of you, and said he simply had to get off. He asked me to say goodbye, and thanks a lot, Marcia, and good luck to you, Mike. Paul and I are nearly through now. He's just done clearing his stuff from the lab.'

'Are you heading for London?' Marcia asked.

'Oh no, it just isn't worth grinding along in the Saturday traffic jams for only two nights at home. The Crowncliff Fortnight starts on Tuesday, you see, so that means clocking in on Monday evening. We're going to make our way there in slow stages, camping in the bus near somewhere where we can get a meal. You can't run to hotels on what Horner pays.'

'I don't think I've left the lab in too bad a mess,' Paul King said, coming up and joining them. 'Blimey, this is the best moment of the whole bloody Fortnight, isn't it? How on earth can you stick a resident job for a whole term on end, Marcia?'

'I get completely browned off at times,' she admitted, 'but there are points. The holidays, for instance, and the money. Residence pays hand over fist these days, with the cost of living rocketing.'

'All the same, a couple of weeks of community life's about our limit,' Janice said. 'Not that we don't appreciate all you've done for us here, Marcia. It's been positively lush compared with what we usually get.'

'Hear, hear,' agreed her husband. 'Don't get me wrong, Marcia. It's just that I'm not the gregarious type. Goodbye, and the best of luck.' He wrung her hand warmly, and swung himself into the driver's seat of the dormobile. 'See you all too soon at Crowncliff, Mike.'

Janice got in beside him, and they drove off, waving as they rounded the corner of the school buildings.

'You ought to be getting a weekend off, too,' Marcia said to Michael Jay. 'Considering your status in Horner's, it seems a bit much that you've got to hare down to Cornwall to see how some wretched holiday camp is ticking over.'

'Comes of being an executive. It's our hectic time of year, you know.'

'Will Geoff be at Crowncliff?' she asked, her mind reverting to Wendy Shaw.

'No. He only does the Fortnight in this area in his summer holidays because he lives near, and knows it so well. I wish I'd had a word with him, just to set your mind at rest over this business, darling, but honestly, you know, we can wash him right out. He may be a bit uncouth, but he's a decent lad and sensible, too. He would never have risked queering Wendy's pitch with Eddy...'

Susan Crump was the next to leave, and finally Michael himself drove off, leaving Marcia feeling desperately blank. At the same time she recognized that she was grateful for a breathing space. So much had happened that she knew she needed to take her bearings. Also, there was a lot of work to be done before she could resume her interrupted holiday. With this in mind, she went purposefully up to the linen room, and was not best pleased to be tracked down there by Andrew Medlicott, looking tense.

'They've all cleared off, I take it?' he said. 'I expect you've heard about that girl disappearing from the Horner establishment. George Bond told me Pike had been here. Did you gather any details? This sort of thing's so bad for a school, happening right on our doorstep.'

Marcia unwillingly gave a third résumé of her telephone conversation with Eddy Horner.

Andrew was appalled. Anxiety furrows etched themselves deeply between his eyes as he listened.

'I hope to God nobody from the crowd who've been staying here was mixed up in it,' he exclaimed.

'I don't see how anyone from here could have gone off with her,' Marcia replied. 'They were all present and correct

31

this morning, and she hadn't come back. She may have by now, of course.'

He continued to sit on the edge of the linen table, his hands in his pockets, and not looking at her.

'Suppose she's been murdered,' he said at last.

'Really, Andrew, you're absolutely morbid,' Marcia exploded, reacting with anger to cover her discomfort at hearing her own secret fear put into words. 'If she took her coat and handbag, obviously she went off with someone she knew. A boy she knows at college, or at home, I expect. It looks as though she meant to be back before the family, and something went wrong, like a car breakdown, and she felt too ashamed to face them.'

She seized a pile of pillow cases and began to count them, embarrassed by her outburst.

'I heard another bit of bad news this morning,' Andrew volunteered after a pause.

'You're a positive ray of sunshine today, aren't you? What was it?'

'Don Glover's got an option on that big field that slopes up behind his caravan site, and is applying for planning permission to put up permanent chalets and a shop, and God knows what. Just imagine what it would look like.'

Marcia groaned.

'How utterly ghastly! He mayn't get planning permission, though. The Residents' Association will fight like mad.'

'It's the wire-pulling behind the scenes. I suppose he's up to the neck in it. I wondered why we'd been spared the usual barging in during the holidays.'

'You're probably right there. Look here, Andrew, shall we go round the place now, and check up on any damage we can claim for from Horner's? The cleaners are coming in on Monday morning.'

This diversionary tactic worked. They went together to inspect all rooms used by the Fortnighters. An enthusiastic preserver of specimens had upset a bottle of spirit over a table, taking off the polish, but apart from this lapse, the recent inmates seemed to have been a careful crowd. Andrew went off to compose a claim, and Marcia hurried back to the linen room.

During the morning the Bonds had moved back into the school, and at lunchtime she learnt that Mr Horner had gone up to some place near Stoneham, to see Wendy Shaw's mother, and that the coastguards had been alerted. There were no further developments during the afternoon. She worked energetically to keep her mind off her anxieties, and finally went to bed in a more tranquil mood after Michael had rung her from Cornwall at extravagant length.

Sunday also passed peacefully. The rain had stopped at last, and during the afternoon she put her accounts aside, and went for a brisk buffeting walk along the beach. The sky was clearing, and the return of the sun diverted her thoughts to her own future with its incredible prospects of happiness.

Monday morning dawned clear and calm, with the first nip of autumn in the air. As she went downstairs after an early breakfast, the morning's mail came through the letterbox with a clatter. Sorting it in the hall, she came on a letter addressed to herself in Michael's clear firm handwriting. She paused with it in her hand with a sense of emotion. How different from Stephen's hasty scrawl, and yet bringing just that same warmth of knowing you mattered...Moved by a sudden impulse she took the letter out into the garden to read. It was little more than a note, brief but loving, written in the car soon after he had left, and posted locally to ensure its arrival this morning. Marcia read it through several times, and then stood gazing out over the sea, marvelling at her happiness. Once again a spring tide was racing up the beach, the tumbling creaming breakers an aftermath of the weekend's rough weather. After a time she became aware that something was lacking. The next moment she realized that in spite of the state of the tide, Sir Toby Belch was completely silent. Astonished, she walked towards the small hollow, partly filled with fragments of rock and encircled by a low railing. What on earth could have stopped the familiar booming of the waves as they broke in the cave below, and the watery hiccups?

An appalling idea occurred to her.

'It isn't the sort of publicity we want for the school, I agree,'
Philip Cary said, 'but the situation could be far worse. Merci-
fully, there isn't the remotest possibility of the body having
been put into the cave from our end of the blowhole shaft :
as you know, it's a mere crack in the rock. Obviously the
poor girl was washed round the headland and into the cave
by the rough seas we've had over the weekend—it's the
normal set of the current. What the police are on to is how
she came to be in the water.'

'Will the inquest be here, in the village?' Andrew Medlicott asked.

'Yes, it has to be. It'll be adjourned, of course. The PM's
being done in Winnage this afternoon, and they'll fix the time
of the inquest afterwards. I hope very much we'll be able to
keep you out of it, Mrs Makepeace, but that rests with Superintendent Crookshank, the Stoneham CID chap. I'm going
over this afternoon—to Winnage, I mean—and I'll try to
have a word with him, and look in here on my way back.'

'I suppose it's only a matter of hours before the Press get
on to us, Mr Cary?' Marcia said, visited by unpleasant
memories of events at the time of Stephen's fatal car accident.

'I'm afraid it is, either in person, or by telephone. When
they do, simply say that the girl was nothing whatever to do
with the school, and try to push them off on to Mr Horner.
He's had plenty of experience of newsmen. If they've cot-
toned on to the fact that the blowhole opens into our grounds,
better take them along to see it for themselves. They'll soon
realize that there's no access from our end. If parents ring up,
you can be a bit more expansive. I suggest that you and
Bond are around this afternoon, Medlicott, in case anything
crops up. And now I'd better be off.'

When he had gone, Andrew Medlicott, taking his respon-
sibilities seriously, asked if he could be given some lunch
and went off to telephone his wife and find George Bond.
Marcia was still feeling shaken by the events of the morning,
and quite glad at the prospect of male support. If only

Michael were not on the road to Crowncliff and inaccessible, she thought, as she went towards the kitchen. He was going to ring her in the evening, but it seemed a long time to wait.

The afternoon dragged intolerably. A couple of local press representatives arrived, and were successfully diverted to Uncharted Seas. A few members of the public appeared in the grounds, and were summarily ejected by George Bond. The crowd which had gathered outside the cave to watch the police taking photographs gradually dispersed.

It was after six when Philip Cary returned. As she came downstairs Marcia saw that he looked grave, and felt a chill of apprehension. At the same moment Andrew appeared from his office. Philip Cary indicated the library.

'I'm afraid there's been a very serious development,' he told them. 'She had been strangled—manually—before going into the water.'

Marcia gave an uncontrollable gasp.

'Had she—' Andrew began.

'No, she hadn't been sexually assaulted or robbed. A gold chain and cross hadn't been taken from her neck, at least. So far there's no sign of the handbag. She was wearing her coat, which possibly suggests that she went out voluntarily. All rather odd features, added to which there's the complication of so many people having cleared out on Saturday. They had a short conference, and the Chief Constable's calling in Scotland Yard. There's not much hope of keeping the school's name out of the papers now, I'm afraid, so it's fortunate for us that the Yard's sending Miss Dennis's nephew down.'

Andrew Medlicott exclaimed. Marcia looked blankly at Philip Cary.

'Why, Detective-Superintendent Pollard,' he said. 'One of the Yard's aces. Didn't you know?'

5

This line of scarlet thread.
Book of Joshua. Chapter 2 verse 5

On this Monday evening the train from Paddington arrived at Stoneham station punctually at 10.10 pm. Among the couple of dozen passengers who alighted were Detective-Superintendent Tom Pollard and Detective-Inspector Gregory Toye of New Scotland Yard. They joined the small straggling procession to the barrier. Here a dark man with a prominent nose and saturnine cast of countenance came forward, and introduced himself as Superintendent Crookshank of the Glintshire CID.

Pollard instantly smelt caginess. This impression built up during the short drive to police headquarters, and the opening stage of the conference with Henry Landfear, Chief Constable of Glintshire, a massive man whose light grey suit gave the impression of being under strain. He sat poker-faced, while Superintendent Crookshank made a bleakly factual statement. Names which would soon fill out into flesh and blood, bricks and mortar, flickered in and out of it. While Pollard's retentive mind registered these, he cast about for a means of making a breakthrough in communication.

'Hold on a minute, Super,' he interrupted. 'Remember Inspector Toye and I are poor ignorant Londoners. What in heaven's name is a blowhole?'

Henry Landfear showed his first sign of animation, and entered the conversation.

'Interesting coastal feature. Several examples in these parts.

36

Rocks have planes of weakness—joints, to the trade—running roughly vertical and horizontal. Under stress the rocks fracture along 'em. On coasts the fractures get enlarged through compression of air when waves smash against cliff faces. Now and again you get a horizontal passage leading to a vertical shaft opening out at the top of the cliff. Then at high tide air's blown clean through, and you hear splashing and booming noises, and sometimes jets of spray are thrown out.'

'Thanks, that couldn't be clearer,' Pollard said. 'What's the diameter of these shafts in the Kittitoe specimen?'

'Nowhere more than six inches,' Crookshank replied, in response to a nod from Henry Landfear. 'So that rules out the body having been put into the cave from the top of the cliff. Judging from the PM report, there doesn't seem to be any doubt that it was washed up on this morning's high spring tide, and lodged at the back of the cave, where it blocked the blowhole affair and stopped the thing making its usual row. That's what struck this Mrs Makepeace at the school—the blowhole opens into their grounds, you see—and she had the gump to get on to Constable Pike.'

'I get you,' said Pollard. 'Sorry to have butted in. Do carry on.'

When the catalogue of facts came to an end he leant back in his chair, clasping his hands behind his head.

'Well, one thing,' he remarked, 'at least you've had us in at the start.'

There was a brief astonished silence, followed by a perceptible thaw. Henry Landfear grinned unexpectedly, and ceased to be a formidable hulk.

'Glad you see it that way,' he replied, reaching for a box of cigarettes and circulating it. 'We expected you'd react as if we were a bad smell. I know it looks as though we dragged our feet at first. It's nearly seventy-two hours since Wendy Shaw was reported missing, but what the hell? You can't start up a murder hunt every time a bird walks out on her job.'

Pollard agreed heartily.

'I've had a case involving a disappearance from a holiday area in August before,' he went on. 'It adds enormously to the

37

difficulties when you've got masses of people on the move. Constable Pike seems to have acted very sensibly. You say that he went up to the Horner bungalow at once, although it was the middle of the night, and checked that there were no signs of forcible entry or a struggle, and that the girl's coat and handbag were missing. Then, when she hadn't returned by first thing on Saturday morning, he contacted his superiors at Winnage, and was ordered to get going on local enquiries, which he promptly did. Meanwhile her home was contacted, and the coastguards alerted. All in order. I suppose,' he added a little cautiously, aware of getting nearer the bone, 'the body was too knocked about after a rough weekend in the sea for the signs of strangulation to be obvious from the start?'

'This is it,' replied Henry Landfear a shade hastily. 'It's a savage sort of coast round there, as you'll see for yourself. Reefs like the teeth of a saw, colossal cliffs, loose shingle— the lot. And, as you say, a rough weekend with a big sea running. The poor kid took a fearful bashing, Crookshank says.'

'Multiple injuries, including fracture of the skull and facial bones, and lacerations and heavy bruising,' Superintendent Crookshank reeled off. 'The police surgeon—that's Dr Luke of Winnage—was suspicious about the bruising in the region of the throat right away, but under the circumstances he felt an expert should be brought in.'

'Morton, who's the Home Office pathologist here, went down,' the Chief Constable took up, continuing the defence of Dr Luke, 'and confirmed that manual strangulation, almost certainly by a man from the size of the marks, was the cause of death. All the other injuries were due to the body being knocked about in the sea. His detailed report will be through tomorrow. The inquest's being opened at two o'clock, down at Kittitoe, by the way. Of course, getting Morton along held things up a bit.'

'Yes, of course.' Mentally cursing the delay arising from Dr Luke's determination to pass the buck, Pollard asked about the probable time of death.

'Morton will only go as far as to say that, in his opinion, the body had been in the sea for at least forty-eight hours.'

38

'Which could mean that she was done and chucked into the water during Friday night. The fact that Mr Horner didn't get an answer when he rang her from here about 10.15 pm suggests that she'd at any rate left the bungalow by then, doesn't it? Of course, we've got to reckon with tides and local currents. I don't expect you've had a chance of getting on to the coastguards yet?'

'Not yet, we haven't.' Superintendent Crookshank produced a large-scale map. 'This'll give you some idea of the place. The bungalow's just here.'

Pollard and Toye studied the map with interest. North of Beckon Head the flat sandy beach of Biddle Bay stretched northwards for about a mile and a half, ending at the town of the same name, a much larger place than Kittitoe. South of the headland the coastline was lower, consisting for some miles of beaches and sand dunes.

'She must have gone in off Beckon Head surely?' Pollard said. 'I mean, beaches simply aren't on for getting bodies into the sea unless you've got a boat. They'd just be carried up again on the next high tide.'

Inspector Toye's pale solemn face peered over his shoulder.

'There's Biddle Head,' he pointed out with habitual caution, indicating a smaller headland to the north.

'Bit far for the body to shift round in time, I'd say,' replied Superintendent Crookshank. 'Matter for the coastguards, though.'

'We'll get on to them tomorrow morning,' Pollard said still scrutinizing the map. 'What did you make of the set-up at the bungalow?' he went on, putting it down.

'Horner's like most chaps who've made money in a big way. Everything must be dropped when he calls out. You know the type. What the hell are you police doing, sitting around on your backsides instead of finding the girl? He swore black and blue that Wendy Shaw would never have gone off leaving the kid on its own. But broad and long he struck me as a decent old chap,' Crookshank allowed. 'He was badly cut up about the murder. His daughter's another cup of tea. She was so hopping mad about her baby being left that she was blackguarding Wendy Shaw, and saying she wouldn't stay in the house with her when she turned up again. Had quite a breeze with her Dad in front of me. This was Saturday morning, of course, before the murder came out.'

'I suppose,' Pollard said reflectively, 'Horner and his daughter didn't bump off the girl themselves? We've only their word for it that they left her alive when they went off in the car on Friday evening, and what happened when they got back.'

'Exactly,' said Henry Landfear, lighting another cigarette. 'The same thought hit us, and we've made a few enquiries. The upshot of these is that they did go off from Kittitoe about seven—Pike happened to see their car going through the village. And we've checked that they dined here as they say, and the London train was half an hour late, and they did meet Mrs Townsend's husband off it. As for any motive for killing Wendy Shaw, we know absolutely nothing. I must say the idea seems pretty far-fetched.'

'I agree. All the same, we'll get these people's private lives vetted, unless by a stroke of luck somebody contacted Wendy Shaw after they'd left...I suppose the rain's put paid to any hope of footprints or tyre tracks outside the bungalow?'

'This is it,' replied Crookshank gloomily. 'It belted down all Friday night, and the best part of Saturday. I've had a couple of chaps going over the garden and the drive this afternoon, and there isn't a hope in hell.'

Pollard returned to the map.

'Is this big building at a lower level the school?'

'That's right. St Julitta's, where Mrs Makepeace works. She's the housekeeper.'

'No one else much there in the middle of August, I suppose?'

'Sorry to disillusion you,' Henry Landfear said, 'but there were about ninety people in residence on Friday night. The place had been let for some course or other, run by Horner's Holidays, incidentally. And barring Mrs Makepeace, the whole damn lot of 'em cleared off on Saturday morning. Over and above that there was the usual Saturday turnover of visitors.'

'Don't make it too easy, will you?' replied Pollard. 'Any more body blows before you push off?'

40

'That's about the sum total up to date. No doubt you'll come in for some more. We're damn glad to unload the job on to you, aren't we, Crookshank? I needn't say we'll do our best to lay on any help you want.'

The conference broke up amicably, the Chief Constable driving the Yard pair to their hotel.

Here a friendly night porter produced a pot of tea.

'I wouldn't have thought it was all that of a case, compared with some we've had,' Toye remarked, putting down his cup after a series of satisfying gulps. 'Just endless fiddling enquiries, and following up dozens of dud leads until we hit the right chap. Clear enough, isn't it, that Wendy Shaw either had a psychopath chum at home or at college, or had picked one up at Kittitoe? She knew that she'd be alone for a few hours on Friday evening, and they'd planned a short run in his car. They must have had a row which ended up in him throttling her, poor kid. I expect she wasn't permissive enough. But anyway, people must have seen them around together before Friday evening. There's the photo of the girl in the file which Crookshank got from her home, and we'll piece together a description of the chap in time, and get an Identikit picture knocked up.'

Pollard was silent for a brief space as he poured himself out another cup of tea.

'All horse sense on your part, old man, but I've got a tiresome hunch that it's not going to be as straightforward as all that. Why, I don't quite know. Possibly something to do with old Horner swearing that she'd never have gone off leaving the baby. There are quite a lot of girls who'd have jibbed at it, you know, even these days.'

'I'll take that for true, sir. All the same, he wouldn't be the first elderly gent to be taken in by a young girl.'

'That's equally true. Quite obviously, one of our first jobs is to find out what sort of a girl Wendy Shaw really was. I'd like to start off with her home and her mother, as it's so near here, but we'd better visit the scene of the crime first, as the detective novelists call it. Anyway, there's the inquest at two. Let's have a quick look through the file, and then turn in.'

Half an hour later Pollard settled into a comfortable bed

41

in a quiet room, but found sleep elusive...Suppose, he thought, Horner isn't an old fool over girls, and Wendy Shaw really was a dependable conscientious type? Either there must have been some signs of a struggle in the bungalow which the family obliterated, deliberately or accidentally, or the murderer somehow tricked her into leaving the place with him. Could he have hammered on the door, and said someone had been taken ill in the drive? She might have stopped to throw on a coat as it was pouring with rain, but what about the handbag? And if he'd gone back to collect the handbag after killing her, with the idea of making it look as though she'd gone out on a jaunt, surely he'd have had to churn up her room a bit while looking for it?

Pollard shut his eyes, was distracted by inexplicable coloured patterns in the darkness, and opened them again.

According to the file, Wendy had said that she was going to collect her supper on a tray, and watch television in the sitting room of the bungalow. Suppose a thief had got in through a window, or the garden door which had been found unlocked, and she'd heard and disturbed him? He might have lost his head, panicked and strangled her. But would a chap of this type have suddenly become collected enough to lay a false trail by removing her coat and handbag, and take the risk of getting her body out of the bungalow and into the sea? And pull off all this without leaving a trace? Unless the Horners were lying, of course—but why the hell should they lie if the murder were nothing whatever to do with them?

This sort of sheer speculation is getting nowhere, Pollard thought, rolling over on to his other side. The only sensible jumping-off ground is the girl herself. His mind ran ahead, drawing up a schedule for the next day...first, the mortuary at Winnage, on the way down...Constable Pike...Uncharted Seas...coastguards...the Shaw home...In that order, unless anything unforeseen turned up.

This programme settled, his mind at last switched itself off, and within minutes he was asleep.

Before they left for Kittitoe the next morning, Pollard rang the Yard. He set in motion an enquiry into the affairs of

Mr Edward Horner, his daughter and son-in-law. He also arranged for a statement to be taken from the latter on the events of Friday night from the time of his arrival at Stoneham.

On the drive down he told Toye to make a détour to Winnage. Here he found the visit to the mortuary emotive rather than informative: the sea had effectively removed all facial clues to Wendy Shaw's personality. Only a pathetic anonymity remained, and he felt deep anger against her killer. Signing to the constable in attendance to replace the sheet over her body, he turned his attention to the small heap of her personal belongings. Her clothes, which were of the cheap mass-produced type, had been carefully dried. The coat was a scarlet anorak, now much discoloured by sea-water and badly torn, with stained wadding protruding from the rents.

'No watch,' Toye remarked.

'It could have been ripped off in the sea, I suppose. Not likely to have been stolen by the murderer: hardly worth taking, judging from her clothes.'

Twenty minutes later the police car provided by Stoneham came over the crest of the hill behind Kittitoe. Toye slowed down, and drew in to the side.

'Good spot,' Pollard said. 'Beckon Head's spectacular, if you like.'

Toye sat contemplating it in silence.

'Canst thou draw out leviathan with an hook?' he quoted abstractedly.

Pollard turned and gaped at him.

'Vicar's text last Sunday,' Toye explained in hurried confusion. 'Difficulties of the present time,' he added, slightly pink.

'My dear chap, there couldn't be a better description. Just look at those contorted rocks looking like muscles bracing themselves against being yanked up out of the water.'

'Those two buildings nearer in would be the Horner bungalow and the school, I take it?' Toye asked in a tone dismissive of further flights of fancy.

Pollard consulted the map borrowed from Stoneham.

'Yes. And you can just see where the road to Biddle Bay

comes out at the far end of the village. Got it? There are the drives to the bungalow and school branching off from it on the left. Isn't that a footpath running out to the headland between the two properties?'

'Footpath all right,' Toye replied, focusing binoculars. 'It goes out to what could be a coastguard's lookout.'

'Here, let me have a go…Yes, I see. My God, what a ghastly caravan park over on our left. Somebody beat Enterprise Neptune to it, worse luck. We'd better push on. I asked Stoneham to ring Pike and say we'd be turning up about now.'

The Kittitoe police house was spruce, having been recently repainted. Its garden was ablaze with zinnias and petunias.

'I shouldn't mind this chap's job,' Pollard remarked, as they went up the path. 'Minimal responsibility, and the tempo of life dead slow.'

Once again, they met with caginess at first, but once reassured that the Yard had not come to criticize his course of action at the onset of the case, Constable Pike relaxed and became communicative.

'How were Mr Horner and Mr and Mrs Townsend reacting to Wendy Shaw's disappearance when you went up in the middle of Friday night?' Pollard asked.

'I could see Mr Townsend was thinking the way I was, sir,' Pike told him. 'I mean, that the girl'd gone out with a boy friend, meaning to be back in good time, and they'd had a mishap of some sort. He backed me up when I suggested ringing round, so I got on to the hospitals, and Winnage station to the officer on duty, and to an all-night garage over at Biddle, but none of 'em knew anything of a smash or a breakdown. That sent Mr Horner into a real taking. He swore she'd never have gone off and left the baby of her own free will. Mrs Townsend was that wild that the kiddy had been left that she was fair blowing her top, and saying if Wendy Shaw ever crossed the threshold again, she'd walk out, and take the baby with her.'

'Did you know Wendy Shaw by sight?'

'Barely, sir,' Pike replied regretfully. 'She hadn't been down here long, to start with, and they stay up at the bungalow most times when the place is packed out as it is in the holiday season. I caught sight of her passing in Mr Horner's car once or twice, or doing a bit of shopping in the village, but to be truthful I'm not sure that I'd've recognized her on her own.'

'It's not surprising,' Pollard said. 'Sun goggles and hair over your face and mass-produced beachwear don't exactly help identification. What do the local people think of Mr Horner, and his daughter?'

Here again, the constable's information was mainly negative. Mr Horner was away most of the time, seeing to his business up in London. He didn't take any part worth mentioning in local affairs, although he'd always put his hand in his pocket for a good cause. The bungalow was more like his holiday home. He was liked well enough, but didn't do much entertaining, especially since his daughter got married last year. Mrs Townsend? Well, she hadn't been around a lot, even before she was married. Bit full of herself and spoilt, people thought.

'Who cleans and cooks for Mr Horner?' Pollard asked.

'Mrs Barrow, sir. A very respectable widow woman. She goes up by the day when he's here, and keeps an eye on the place when it's empty. He comes and goes a lot.'

Pollard watched Toye noting down Mrs Barrow's address, and went on to enquire about the local coastguard service. Having gathered that Ted Chugg would be over at the lookout, but came home to dinner at half-past twelve, he decided that Constable Pike's usefulness as a source of information was, at least for the moment, exhausted.

'We'll almost certainly want a lot of help from you over a house-to-house enquiry, Pike,' he told him, 'and I'm glad you're here to carry it out. You coped with this affair very sensibly at the early stages, as I said to the Chief Constable last night. Meanwhile, we'll be getting on to see Mr Horner.'

They drove off a few minutes later, having been ceremoniously escorted to their car.

On the far side of the village they took the road to Biddle Bay, and almost at once bore left into the drive entrance of Uncharted Seas. The gate was closed, and two unmistakable newsmen rose from the hedge to bear down on the car.

'Have a heart,' Pollard adjured them in response to a flood of questions. 'I've only just got here, while you chaps have been hanging around for God knows how long. Haven't you got anything for us?'

There were some good-humoured jeers and exchanges, and he placated them by emphasizing that there was to be an all-out effort to follow up Wendy Shaw's local contacts, and suggesting that they might lend a hand, now that her photograph had been released to the Press. Finally one of them obligingly opened the gate for the car. Toye drove swiftly and steeply upwards until the drive abruptly flattened out on the landward side of a large, solidly built bungalow.

'See that?' Toye demanded, indicating the open doors of a garage. 'A Jag—the XJ6.' A car enthusiast, he gazed longingly.

'This place must have put old Horner back a bit, too,' Pollard said, eyeing Uncharted Seas, and conscious of the mortgage on his London home.

As they disembarked the front door of the bungalow opened. An elderly man, short and tubby, and wearing brown corduroy trousers and a green shirt, stood staring at them uncompromisingly.

'If you're another lot of bloody reporters, beat it,' he said, surprisingly authoritative for his size and build.

The punch behind the Horner empire, Pollard thought as he went forward...

'Good morning, Mr Horner,' he said. 'We're CID officers from New Scotland Yard. I'm Detective-Superintendent Pollard, and this is Detective-Inspector Toye who is working with me on the enquiry into Wendy Shaw's death.'

Eddy Horner's face remained expressionless.

'If the local police blockheads had listened to me, you'd have been down here by midday Saturday. Not that it makes any difference, I suppose, seeing that Wendy was dead by then, from all accounts. You'd better come inside.'

He turned on his heel, and led the way to the long sitting room facing the sea. As he walked, his shoulders sagged a little. The French windows on to the terrace were open, and Pollard could see a young woman sitting beside a baby's pram.

'Scotland Yard,' Eddy Horner called to her. 'My daughter, Mrs Townsend,' he added, as the young woman got up and came into the room. He introduced Pollard and Toye with the minimum of words. She was taller and more lightly built than her father, and very pretty, with long copper-brown hair and big grey eyes. As he sized her up Pollard detected an underlying petulance. Her old man's made the grade by brain and sweat, he thought, while she's come to expect everything on a plate as her right, and sees this business as a sort of personal outrage.

'You'll take something, won't you?' Penny Townsend asked as she shook hands. 'A cup of coffee?'

'Thank you, no,' Pollard replied. 'We're on duty, you see.'

'Better sit down and get on with it then, hadn't we?'

Eddy Horner followed up this remark by dropping into a chair. Pollard deftly manoeuvred Penny into another beside him, and settled himself facing them both. Toye faded into the background, taking out his notebook.

'This stage of the enquiry is always very tiresome for people connected with a case, I'm afraid,' Pollard opened. 'When we take over, we always like to have information at first hand, whether it's already been given or not. I'd like to begin with Wendy Shaw herself. How did she come to be employed here?'

'She was a relative of mine,' Eddy Horner said heavily.

Pollard could not repress an exclamation of surprise, while registering at the same moment a slight movement of impatience by Penny Townsend.

'This fact was not in your original statement, Mr Horner,' he said.

'I don't suppose I thought to mention it. She wasn't a blood relation. Only a distant connection of my late first wife — not Penny's mother, I've been married twice. Mrs Shaw's husband went off with another woman, leaving her with three kids and next to nothing. I've helped out a bit to get 'em educated and able to stand on their own feet. Wendy was training as a children's nurse. Doing very well, the college said.'

'So you had known Wendy for some time, Mr Horner, and are in a position to tell us the kind of girl she was?'

'All this doesn't add up to nearly as much as it sounds,' Penny broke in rather irritably. 'All right, Dad. I know I hit the roof at first, and said things I didn't mean, and the police will have passed them on. I was frightened about what might have happened to baby. What I mean is,' she went on, turning to Pollard, 'sending along some cash, and reading school and college reports doesn't tell you what a person is really like, does it?'

'Only to a limited extent,' he agreed.

'What I'm trying to get across is this,' she went on, shaking back her hair. 'Wendy was a nice enough girl, but she'd had a very drab sort of life at home with a mother who's got an outsize chip on her shoulder, as far as I can make out. Wendy couldn't be blamed for it, of course, but she was hopelessly shy and honestly a bit of a drag to have around all the time. I mean, if we had anyone in for a drink, she simply couldn't utter, and just sat. We tried to get her to join the Youth Club as a holiday member, but it was no go: she was scared stiff at the idea. Then, about two or three weeks ago, she came in from doing some shopping, and said she'd met up with a girl from home, and could she go out with her. Of course, we were thrilled to bits, and pushed it for all we were worth. I told her she could bring the girl up here, but she didn't seem to want to. Of course, it's pretty obvious now that it wasn't a girl friend at all. She'd been picked up by some man, and being so green, poor kid, she wasn't to know he was a real bad hat. Oh, I know she hadn't actually been raped, but still…It sticks out a mile, doesn't it?'

Pollard met her rather aggressive gaze thoughtfully.

'Have you any evidence—I mean evidence that would stand up in a court of law—that this alleged girl friend was, in fact, a man?' he asked.

'No,' she replied, 'unless they'd believe me when I said that she changed after she started going out with whoever it was. Perked up. Came in starry-eyed. Didn't she, Dad?'

Eddy Horner, who had been sitting slumped in his chair, raised his head.

'I reckon Penny's got something there,' he told Pollard. 'Wendy certainly was a bit brighter lately. My God, this business has blown me right off course. I feel as though I fell down on my responsibility for the child while she was in my house, and I'm not a man who defaults, I'd have you know. We ought to have done more to keep her happy.'

'I doubt very much whether you could have,' Pollard replied. 'There's no one more unhelpable than a teenager at some stages. To go back to my first question, I should have expected you to get a more experienced nurse for your first baby, Mrs Townsend.'

'This is it—I did,' she replied, tossing back her hair again. 'I just can't get over the sheer rotten bad luck of it all. I fixed with a first-class college trained nurse to come down here with me at the end of June, and the wretched woman must go and have an acute appendix the day before I came out of the nursing home. It couldn't have been more inconvenient. But I felt she was worth waiting for, and Dad suddenly thought that Wendy would be on holiday, and might tide me over. We knew that she was reasonably capable with babies from her reports. She jumped at it—a chance to get away from home, of course. And to think that the nurse is due to come on Saturday. It's ridiculous, the way she's stuck out for all these weeks of convalescence. People don't think anything of having an appendix out these days. If only she'd been reasonable, all this would never have happened.'

'No,' Pollard could not refrain from saying, 'It wouldn't, and Wendy Shaw would still be alive.'

There was a short silence, in the course of which Penny Townsend looked slightly uncomfortable.

'Mrs Shaw told me she didn't know of any girl friend of Wendy's on holiday down here,' Eddy Horner said suddenly.

'There's a lot most mothers don't know about their daughters' friends these days,' Pollard replied. 'I shall be seeing Mrs Shaw, and enquiries will be made in her neighbourhood, of course. Are you both quite sure that Wendy said she had met a friend from home, and not a college friend?'

Assured on this point, he began to ask questions about the events of Friday evening. Step by step he covered the ground from their departure for Stoneham at approximately seven o'clock, to their delayed return at twenty minutes to twelve. They had found the bungalow in darkness, the television set switched on here in the sitting room, the baby whimpering in its cot, and no sign of Wendy. They had searched in vain for a note explaining her absence, but had found that her coat—a scarlet anorak—and her white plastic handbag were missing. The catch of the Yale lock on the front door was down, as they had left it, but the door at the end of the passage which led into the garden was unlocked. They admitted that this door was often overlooked, and left unsecured all night. There had been no sign of any disturbance inside the bungalow, and nothing was missing other than the coat and bag. Mr Townsend had gone out in the pouring rain and searched the garden and drive, and after ringing the school to ask if Wendy had been seen down there, they had finally contacted Constable Pike.

Aware that these statements tallied with those recorded in the case file, Pollard asked to see over the bungalow. The guest wing was to the right of the front door. It consisted of a large double bedroom occupied by Penny and the baby, a single room which had been Wendy Shaw's, a bathroom and lavatory and a small kitchenette. Wendy's room was comfortable and well-furnished, and she had been provided with an armchair and a transistor radio. All these rooms faced south, being reached by a passage on the north side of the bungalow, which ended in the garden door already mentioned.

Pollard looked at the highly polished parquet floor of the passage.

'I understand that your daily woman cleaned as usual on Saturday morning,' he said.

'How the hell were we to know that it ought to be left?' Eddy demanded with self-accusatory truculence.

'You couldn't reasonably have been expected to at that stage,' Pollard replied, 'especially after Constable Pike had checked up for signs of anything in the way of a break-in. It's unfortunate, as things have turned out, but all cases have their bits of bad luck, and unexpected good luck, too, come to that.' He looked at his watch, and turned to Toye. 'Inspector, if you nip down in the car, I think you'll catch Mr Chugg on his way home for his dinner. Ask him to come up here for a few minutes.'

Toye vanished.

'Chugg's one of the best,' Eddy Horner said heavily. 'If anyone round here can tell you what you want to know, he can.'

Unexpectedly Penny Townsend shivered.

'If you'll excuse me,' she said shakily, 'I ought to be seeing to baby.'

'Could I have a word with your Mrs Barrow?' Pollard asked Eddy.

'Sure. Come this way.'

Pollard followed in the direction of the kitchen. Here a grey-haired woman was preparing lunch. Eddy Horner introduced her, and left them together. To Pollard's amazement she made a birdlike dart at him.

'Excuse me,' she exclaimed, 'A little end of thread caught on your coat.'

The action, he quickly realized, was symptomatic. The driving force of her life was hostility to anything which could be described as dirt or mess. Quite oblivious of what lay behind his questioning, she described with relish the thoroughness of her regular Saturday morning cleaning of Uncharted Seas.

'It 'as to be done proper, seein' as I don't come up Sundays,' she explained. 'I 'ad to leave the outsides of the winders as it was rainin' and blowin', but they got a good do Monday. All caked with salt and sand, they were, after the gale.'

Breaking off, she hurried across to the cooker, and gave the contents of a saucepan a brisk stir.

Pressed as to whether she had noticed anything in the least out of the ordinary when cleaning on Saturday morning, she shook her head emphatically.

'Savin' all the mud and mess they'd brought in Friday night looking for Wendy, pore girl. Nice kiddy she was. Not much to say for 'erself, but I'd rather 'ave it that way meself than all these brazen 'ussies these days. Bit of an innercent, I'd say, and one of these sex maniacs took advantage of 'er. My, if that isn't Ted Chugg with his great boots out there! Not comin' in, is 'e?'

'No,' Pollard reassured her, 'I'm going out to talk to him.

Thank you for your help, Mrs Barrow.'

'Pleased, I'm sure,' she replied perfunctorily, and before he reached the door was back at her saucepans again.

Ted Chugg was a quiet man with intent light blue eyes, surprisingly pale for one who led a largely outdoor life. Pollard slipped into the back of the car, and gave him the gist of the post mortem report on Wendy Shaw.

'You see what I'm getting at,' he concluded. 'We'd like your opinion on where she probably went into the water. As far as we know at present, she was last seen alive—except by the murderer—at seven o'clock on Friday evening, and there was no answer to a phone call made to the bungalow at ten-fifteen. You already know that the body was found in the cave down there about half-past nine on Monday morning.'

Ted Chugg listened and nodded.

'Not much doubt as to where she went in, to my way o' thinkin',' he said. 'Up over.'

He jerked his head in the direction of Beckon Cove.

Pollard gave an exclamation of surprise.

'Why, on the Ordnance map it looks as though the Cove is all but land-locked,' he said. 'I'd have expected anything going in there just to drift around in circles.'

'Take a look, shall us?' suggested the coastguard.

All three men went up the slope behind the bungalow, and stood at the top of a zigzag flight of concrete steps leading down to a crescent of shingle on the east side of Beckon Cove. The narrow outlet to the sea was directly facing this little beach. Immediately below where they were standing the water was deep, and lay in the dark shadow of the Beckon Head ridge. Ted Chugg pointed downwards.

'I reckon the maid was pitched over from yur,' he said. 'Tis this way. There's a current swirls round the Cove clockwise, see? Friday night's ebb'd move a body round towards the gap. Wind shifted westwards durin' the night, and banked up Saturday mornin's flood, makin' for a mighty powerful scour out to sea when the tide turned. As I sees it, she'd be washed out clear of the 'eadland. There's an offshore current out yonder, workin' north to south, and 'twould carry 'er past Beckon, round into Kittitoe Bay, where she'd be carried up the beach on the flood. 'Twas top o' springs over the weekend.'

Pollard, who detested heights, stood well back from the railing on the outside of the steps as he followed the coast-guard's argument.

'I see all that,' he said, 'but why do you think the body was chucked in from here? Wouldn't the same thing have happened in the end from any point off the headland?'

'Kittitoe Bay side, visitors pokin' around would've found'n afore Monday mornin',' Ted Chugg said decisively. 'Off the end o' Beckon—well—'twould be a rare job luggin' a body out there, in the dark, what's more. It don't seem likely to me.'

'Fair enough,' Pollard agreed, looking unhappily at Toye, who was hanging perilously over the railing, and peering downwards.

'Sheer for a good hundred and fifty feet,' the latter said, righting himself. 'And nothing much clothes would have caught on from the look of it. The water's pretty deep down there, isn't it?'

'Round six foot at low tide,' Ted Chugg told him. 'The cliff's undercut a bit, though, an' the current'd carry 'er close in. Shall us go down?'

After Toye had made a fruitless attempt to bring up identifiable fingerprints from the railing, they made the descent to the Cove.

It was surprisingly hot down on the shingle. The high encircling cliffs created an atmosphere of secluded remoteness. Apart from the rhythmic rattle of shingle shifted by the ebbing tide, and the occasional cries of seabirds floating far above, the silence was unbroken. Pollard developed a strong distaste for the place. There was a rank smell of stranded seaweed, and the drifting clouds produced the unpleasant illusion that the cliffs were collapsing inwards.

'Not my cuppa,' Ted Chugg remarked, echoing his thoughts. 'Too shut in, like. Pongs, too. What'll us be lookin' for, sir?'

'Bits of bright red cloth, ripped off an anorak, and possibly bits of the white wadding the thing was padded with. There's a white plastic handbag somewhere, too, unless the murderer took it off with him.'

They walked to the limit of the beach on their left. Ted Chugg began to wade into the water.

'I'll work me way round a bit,' he said. 'It shelves, but there's a foothold so long as you goes steady, an' keeps in close.'

'Can't we get hold of an RAF rubber dinghy, or inflatable raft?' Pollard suggested.

'Bit o' wet don't worry me, sir. I've got me boots on.'

The underwater shingle squeaked and slithered as he progressed, steadying himself against the base of the cliff, and scrutinizing both cliff face and water. Pollard and Toye watched him reach the point immediately below where they had stood at the top of the steps, and pass beyond it. About a dozen yards further on he suddenly stopped, and bent forward. Then, gripping at the cliff with his left hand, he groped under the surface of the water with his right, and hoisted up what looked like a long flat strip of metal. He shouted, but the words were swallowed up in the echo from the cliffs. Turning, he began to retrace his steps, holding his find clear of the water.

'What the hell has he got there?' Pollard demanded. 'It looks like part of a barrel hoop.'

'Could be,' Toye agreed cautiously.

Emerging on to the dry shingle, Ted Chugg held out a rusty flat length of metal, about an inch and a half wide. Caught up on it, and held secure by a scarlet thread was a torn scrap of material of the same colour.

'Wendy Shaw's anorak, all right,' Pollard exclaimed triumphantly, as he examined it with care. 'It'll have to go to the forensic boys for confirmation, but I'd stake my pension on it, wouldn't you, Toye? Man,' he told Chugg, 'this is the first definite lead we've had.'

6

Home is the girl's prison and the
woman's workhouse.
Shaw. Maxims for Revolutionists.

The investigations in Beckon Cove had been time-consuming, leaving no chance of lunch before the inquest. Toye drove Ted Chugg back to his home in the village, and hastily collected up sandwiches and a couple of cans of beer before rejoining Pollard, who had strolled out on the road to Biddle Bay. They ran the car into a layby, and between mouthfuls agreed that Eddy Horner and his daughter were just not on as suspects in the case.

'Of course, I'd like absolute proof that Wendy Shaw was alive when they left for Stoneham,' Pollard said. 'That sort of thing's tidier. But in the meantime one has to use a bit of commonsense. Old Horner's unthinkable as a murderer, and Penny Townsend couldn't possibly have carried the job through single-handed. Anyway, I can't see her taking the risk of committing a murder unless her entire well-being depended on it, perhaps. There's not a shred of evidence that Wendy was any sort of threat to her.'

Toye took another sandwich.

'There's the husband,' he said indistinctly.

'Come off it,' Pollard replied. 'You've seen Wendy's photograph. There's a point beyond which the camera can't lie. Or are you suggesting that Townsend is a homicidal maniac, and his wife and father-in-law are trying to cover for him? Well, we'll soon have the life histories of all three of them through from the Yard, to put your mind at rest. Here, look at the time…We'll be late for the inquest if we don't watch out.'

They slipped into the seats kept for them just before the coroner, a brisk solicitor from Winnage, opened the proceedings. He conducted them so expeditiously that he was driving away again in under half an hour, having seen through the necessary formalities and adjourned the court for a fortnight. The packed village hall emptied rapidly, leaving Pollard and Toye discussing the manpower needed for a house-to-house enquiry in and around Kittitoe with Superintendent Bostock of the Winnage Constabulary. Presently they came out on to the steps, and stood talking for a few minutes longer. By this time all but a handful of curious onlookers had drifted off, and Constable Pike stood surveying the scene with the air of one who had maintained law and order under difficulties. As Superintendent Bostock called to him to come over and hear what had been decided, Pollard noticed a grey-haired, rather distinguished looking man sitting in a Rover drawn up at the kerb. As soon as the Winnage police car departed, the stranger got out and came forward.

'Superintendent Pollard?' he said pleasantly. 'Your aunt, Miss Isabel Dennis, asked me to give you this note. She knew I was coming along to the inquest, and thought it would be the simplest way of getting in touch with you.'

'Very good of you, sir,' Pollard replied, accepting an envelope. 'I take it you're a neighbour of hers?'

'Yes, I live at Holston, too—Philip Cary. We seem to land up on the same committees, as well, including the governing body of St Julitta's school over there. She's a quite invaluable member: never misses a thing.'

Pollard laughed.

'I well believe it,' he said. 'As a small boy I found her a bit overwhelming on occasions. I'm hoping to look in on her, but one simply can't tell what will happen from hour to hour in this sort of job.'

'Ghastly business,' Philip Cary said with feeling. 'I'm more sorry than I can say for Eddy Horner. It isn't too good for the school, either. However, I mustn't waste your time. Good hunting.'

He went off.

56

Pollard ripped open the envelope. Like all communications from his aunt, it was faultlessly typed, this time on a postcard with the printed heading From Miss Isabel Dennis MBE, Cob Cottage, Holston, Stoneham S27 6FZ. Tel Winnage 3485.

24 August 1971

Bed and/or board of course available here for you and Inspector Toye, if this would be helpful at any time.

In case this is relevant, I spoke to Wendy Shaw on the telephone at just before 8.00 pm last Friday evening, when she appeared perfectly normal.

Affectly,
Aunt Is.

'Well anyway, here's definite proof that old Horner and his daughter are out of it,' Pollard said, passing the missive to Toye. 'Much better to clear the decks.'

Toye agreed sombrely, adding that it was very good of Miss Dennis to include him in the invitation, and he appreciated it.

'She's the goods, even if a bit of a tough. Well, this is where we make for Mrs Shaw's, I suppose.'

On the road they discussed progress.

'Let's face it,' Pollard said, 'that bit of anorak—and I'm positive that's what it is—doesn't get us much further. Chugg is an expert witness and says that the body must almost certainly have gone into Beckon Cove. So what? Is there anything in this for us?'

'Doesn't it depend on where the murder took place?' Toye asked.

'Yea. If inside, or just outside the bungalow, or if further afield and the body was brought back in a car, the slope up to the drop to the Cove was the shortest haul to the sea. And on private property, too. The murderer presumably knew that Horner and Penny Townsend were out, and not due back until after eleven. It all focuses attention on the bungalow, doesn't it?'

Toye shot past a small car towing a wobbly caravan.

'All the same,' he said, 'wouldn't most people think anything chucked into the Cove would stay there, just bobbing around? We did, until Chugg explained about the currents and tides. I reckon the murderer would have gone for the open sea, even if it did mean lugging the body along the headland. On a night like last Friday's, you'd hardly be likely to run into anyone.'

'Risky, though. I'm not saying your reasoning isn't sound, but the chap mightn't have had the physical strength to get the body that far. Or he might have panicked, and taken the shortest cut to getting rid of it. This implies, of course, that the murder was unpremeditated. Or he could have been a knowledgeable local up in the current and tides, or just a dim type of landlubber who thought that once he'd dumped the girl in the water, the sea would obligingly transport her to an unknown destination. Or any combination of these.'

'True,' Toye agreed, 'and a mentally disturbed bloke, any-way.'

'This line of thought is just leading us into a bog. Let's consider practical steps. The important thing is to try to trace any person or car seen near Uncharted Seas between eight o'clock and eleven-forty on Friday night, and more particularly before ten-fifteen, when the phone call from Stoneham wasn't answered. Bostock and I impressed this on Pike, and he's getting going on the job at once, with a chap Bostock's sending out from Winnage to help. Meanwhile, you and I get on to Wendy's friends and acquaintances up here through her mother. Step on it as much as you can: I'd hoped to be at Mrs Shaw's by now.'

Half an hour later they turned off the Winnage-Stoneham road for Cotterton, where the Shaws lived. It was a feature-less village, in process of being further depersonalized by gradual absorption into Stoneham, four miles away. After enquiring at the post office they located Marina Road, which was flanked by pairs of semi-detached houses of the inter-war vintage. Number Eight was in need of a facelift, and its patch of front garden consisted of rough grass, ragged shrubs and a few nasturtiums. A car was drawn up at the gate, and as Toye parked behind it, a woman emerged from the front door and stood with her back to them, talking to someone inside.

'...you don't have to worry about those two any more,'

Pollard caught. 'Your cousin won't stand for any nonsense, I could see that. Now...'

The speaker broke off abruptly and turned round at the sound of steps on the path.

'Mrs Shaw isn't—' she began again.

Pollard produced his credentials and introduced himself.

'I'm extremely sorry to have to bother Mrs Shaw at a moment like this,' he told her, 'but I'm afraid I must see her. I'm conducting the official enquiry into her daughter's death. Are you a friend of hers?'

The woman, middle-aged and sensible-looking, hesitated momentarily.

'I've known her for a long time, Mrs Boyd's my name. I'm doing what I can to help. Shall I tell her you're here?'

'Please do,' Pollard replied. He stepped into the house close on her heels.

'...Scotland Yard...seems very kind...look in again later,' he heard.

Intent as he was on his first impression of Mrs Shaw, he registered an exceptionally ugly room, in which the original colour scheme had faded to a depressing overall dun. There were no flowers or signs of relaxed enjoyment such as books or magazines, or a television set.

As he opened the interview with expressions of genuine sympathy, Mrs Shaw puzzled him. She sat twisting her hands, obviously in the grip of a strong emotion which he sensed instinctively was not entirely personal grief at her daughter's appalling death. As he talked, he observed her carefully.

The adjective which leapt to his mind was uncared-for. He placed her in her middle-forties, making due allowance for the ageing effect of badly bobbed straight hair, a neglected complexion without a trace of make-up, and a shapeless skirt and jumper. Her mouth turned down obstinately at the corners. Her hazel eyes—her best feature—had an oddly absorbed look, as if necessary contacts with the external world were an interruption to her private life.

In response to his stock remark about co-operation in tracing Wendy's killer, she seemed to make an effort to concentrate her attention on the immediate present.

'Even if you do find the man, it won't bring Wendy back,' she said dully. 'If only she'd taken that holiday job in Stoneham, instead of going to Cousin Eddy. It was the money, of course. That, and being under an obligation...'

Pollard intuitively seized on money as the operative word. In response to an adroit question, the all-too-familiar story of desertion and its financial implications came pouring out with an almost startling bitterness. He listened to a chronicle of hardship which struck him as barely credible in view of the welfare state, and the connection with Eddy Horner. I believe it's been her way of hitting back at the humiliation of being deserted, and probably quite unconsciously at the sexual deprivation it's involved, he thought. It helped to flaunt the financial insecurity the husband inflicted on her, and she's gone on wallowing in it until she's come to believe in it as a permanent fact of life...

'I understand Mr Horner has helped with the children's education?' he shot at her.

In confirmation of his theory she gave him a look of angry resentment, and ignored the implied question, continuing her tirade on the ever-increasing cost of living, and the problem of keeping the home going.

He decided to come to the main purpose of his visit.

'Mrs Shaw,' he said, 'Wendy told Mr Horner, as you probably already know, that she had met a girl friend from home who was on holiday in Kittitoe, and had been seeing something of her. We're anxious to get in touch with this girl. You see, Wendy might have told her about other contacts she'd made. I expect Wendy mentioned it in her letters to you. Can you give us the girl's name and address?'

Once again, Mrs Shaw reacted angrily.

'It's rubbish,' she said. 'I don't believe a word of it. There isn't a girl round here who'd go about with Wendy on holiday. I hadn't the money to give her for the clothes and stuff to put on her face they all have these days.'

'Come now, Mrs Shaw,' Pollard said patiently, 'even if they weren't close friends Wendy must have known local girls she went to school with. Stoneham High School, wasn't

60

it? Quite natural that if she met one of them down there they should have spent time together.'

'You can't know much about present-day teenagers,' she said contemptuously. 'Any girl like Wendy who comes from a home where every penny has to do the work of two is right out of things. Pounds a week these girls round here fritter away. Besides, holidays at Kittitoe wouldn't be grand enough for the parents of most of them. It's got to be the Costa Brava, or going on cruises. What we've got to live on doesn't run to holidays at all.'

There was a brief pause during which steps were audible on the path, and something clattered through the letter box.

'Well, if Wendy hadn't any girl friends, what about boy friends?' Pollard asked.

This time, Mrs Shaw looked frightened.

'Wendy wasn't interested in boys,' she said hastily. 'Her home was what mattered to her, and helping me. She was only eleven when her father went off and left us, and she's shared all the awful worry with me. We've been more like two sisters. She understood I couldn't give her what other girls had. All she wanted was to get a decent job, and bring a bit of money in to make things easier. Nothing else would have made her go away to a training college.'

God help the unfortunate girl, if all this is true, Pollard thought. I suppose the training college may have opened her eyes a bit…

'Where are your younger children, Mrs Shaw?' he asked, suddenly visited by the idea of getting sidelights on Wendy's social contacts in Cotterton through conversation with them.

An ugly red suffused Mrs Shaw's face.

'I've sent them away where they can't be badgered by the police or the papers,' she said. 'And I'm not telling anyone— anyone—where they are.'

Her voice rose slightly. After looking at her thoughtfully, Pollard got to his feet.

'I don't think we need inflict ourselves on you any longer, then,' he told her.

She made no reply, but followed the two men to the front door. Pollard picked up a parish magazine from the mat, and handed it to her. She almost snatched it from his hand.

'You needn't think we can afford to take in magazines,' she said shrilly. 'This one's passed on.'

'If I can help you, Mrs Shaw,' he said, pausing on the step, 'you have only to ring the Stoneham police station, or ask Mrs Boyd or another friend to ring for you.'

Her only reply was to slam the door after them, and turn the key.

'God, what a psychological mess,' he exclaimed, getting into the car and banging the door. 'Martyrdom as a substitute for matrimony. It's those three unfortunate kids one thinks of.'

'Why did you let her off the hook, sir?' Toye enquired. 'Refusing information,' he added indignantly.

'I didn't want to cope with a bout of hysterics, and we can easily find out from Mrs Boyd where the younger ones are. She'd obviously taken them there from what she was saying when we arrived. I rather think there's been a break-out. Remember what she said about the cousin not standing any nonsense?'

'That's true. And she was somehow angry at the mention of them. Where to, sir?'

'The Vicarage, I think. The Rev. Charles Vention can probably fill in a few gaps, if she's involved with the church to the extent of having the parish mag passed on. I spotted his name on the outside of the thing. This session with Mrs Shaw has been quite useful, you know.'

'Meaning that it bears out what Mrs Townsend said about Wendy being shy and a dead loss at a party?'

'Yes, and inexperienced enough to get herself picked up by a wrong 'un. And the fact that she obviously hadn't mentioned the alleged girl friend in her letters home rather suggests that something of this sort had happened. Any idea of her heading in the direction of matrimony would have sent her mother sky high: she'd certainly have had the sense to keep quiet about acquiring a boy friend. Here we are, I think.'

Cotterton's Victorian vicarage was set in a huge rambling garden. Although largely out of control, the latter was brilliantly colourful with patches of rampant dahlias. The front door bell was apparently out of order, but vigorous hammering brought a cheerful youngish woman in slacks from the back regions.

'Good grief!' she exclaimed at the sight of Pollard's card. 'None of our lot's been up to anything really awful, I hope. Do come in. The kitchen, if you don't mind. We always eat there, and are just finishing high tea. It's the PCC tonight.'

A lavish use of bright colour, and a display of modern decorative posters had converted the cavernous kitchen into a welcoming lived-in room. The far end had been converted into a dining area, and as they came in, a man of about forty-five got up from the table, wiping his mouth. He had a thin alert face, and an unruly shock of hair.

'If you're Scotland Yard,' he said, after his wife had carried out introductions, 'something tells me you're here in connection with this ghastly business of poor little Wendy Shaw.'

'You're quite right,' Pollard replied. 'We've just come from Mrs Shaw.'

'Join us in a cup of coffee, won't you, and tell us if there's anything we can do?'

Pollard accepted a large steaming cup of coffee, and embarked on an account of his recent interview.

'All one's been able to do about Mrs Shaw,' Charles Vention said reflectively when the narrative came to an end, 'is to circumvent her as far as possible over the girls. She is, as you say, a psychological mess. It's true there isn't much money, but the family certainly isn't on the breadline. The husband pays something in the way of maintenance, there are the Social Security allowances, and Mr Horner allows her a certain amount as well. In addition she now has a part-time job in a big store in Stoneham. I absolutely agree with your diagnosis. We think that she's cultivated this struggling martyr role as a means of somehow asserting her identity, which she felt was threatened when she lost her status as a normally married woman. The way the human mind works is baffling beyond words, isn't it? But of course it's been disastrous for the children. It didn't matter so much when they were younger. People were awfully good in asking them out, and giving them treats, and their age groups took them for granted, as the young do at that stage. But when they became teenagers, it began to be another story. If you haven't the in-gear, and aren't able to do your thing, well, I'm afraid you're out. Wendy has retreated into a shell and become quite dumb, and even going away to college hasn't seemed to do much for her. She remained hopelessly immature. Is this the sort of gen you want, by the way?'

'Very much so. How was Mrs Shaw persuaded to let her go?'

'It was a conspiracy between my husband and the head-mistress of the High School,' Mrs Vention told Pollard. 'He persuaded her to write to Mr Horner, and of course, he was in a position to put pressure on Mrs Shaw.'

'Wendy doesn't seem to have told her mother about any contacts she made in Kittitoe. Does this surprise you?'

'Not in the least,' Charles Vention replied. 'Mrs Shaw clung to Wendy even more than to the others. They were an essential part of her fantasy life, you see. She sees herself working like a slave to keep the family together, while they react with adoring gratitude, and everybody else is an also-ran. Wendy no doubt realized all this, and would certainly have been cagey about her first steps in the direction of a life of her own. Sonia's going to be a very different proposition. She managed to slip out and contact a reporter yesterday, and sold him a school photograph of Wendy for a fiver. She then took the next bus into Stoneham, and blew the lot. She's sixteen. Ann, the youngest, is thirteen, and they've both been packed off to some elderly relative pro tem.'

'I see,' said Pollard. 'That explains the reaction when I asked to see them. I thought I might get something out of them about Wendy's friends here. Mrs Shaw insisted that she hadn't any, as it was impossible for them to keep up with the Joneses.'

'There's a certain amount of truth in that,' Mrs Vention remarked, looking up from something she was writing. 'But I can think of quite half a dozen girls who would have been decent to her if they'd run into her at Kittitoe. I've been jotting down their names and addresses for you. As far as I know, though, none of them has been on holiday down there, but you'll be able to check on this, won't you? Wendy was in the same year as our daughter Hilary, so we know the crowd pretty well. Wendy was tending to drop out of things, especially since she went off to college, but her contemporaries respected her, as well as being sorry for her. Hilary made a point of having her round here, and so on.'

'Sorry Hilary isn't available,' Charles Vention said. 'She's putting in six months on a kibbutz in Israel before going up to the university. Back in three weeks, thank goodness.'

'Here she is.'

Mrs Vention handed Pollard a photograph of a girl absurdly like her father, her face full of vitality and intelligence.

'Have you any family?' she asked.

'Assorted twins,' Pollard told her. 'Meet Andrew and Rose Pollard, aged two years and eight months. This very day they're being interviewed for places in a play group.'

Mrs Vention pounced on the snapshot from his wallet with a delighted exclamation.

Later, after a well-earned meal at their Stoneham hotel, Pollard persuaded Toye to take the rest of the evening off.

'Look what's on at the Odeon,' he said, taking up an evening paper. 'The Tomahawk Thunder Trail—real full-blooded stuff. Just your cuppa. If you push off now, you'll get in for the last house.'

After Toye had gone off to indulge his surprising passion for Westerns, Pollard made for a telephone kiosk, and rang his wife.

Her voice came excitedly over the line.

'They've both been accepted for September! Isn't it super? People aren't supposed to know until tomorrow, but Mrs Lind whispered to me when I went to fetch them. Apparently, they stared at the ones who howled, and made themselves completely at home investigating the equipment. They even asked intelligibly to be taken to the loo.'

'The first step on the educational ladder has been achieved, in fact.'

'Come off it, darling! What I'm thinking of is a gorgeous spot of free time each morning for shopping or a hair do, or just pottering. How are things going?'

'We haven't done much driving today,' he said, using

their motoring code. 'Just running around at this stage...'

Much cheered by this contact with home, he went out of the hotel in search of the nearest open space. Strolling round an uninspired public park, he was unable to keep his mind off the case. At any rate, Wendy Shaw had emerged as a person. A pathetic one, stunted by the pressures brought to bear on her by her mother's curious mental state. But certainly a person with a sense of loyalty and duty. This was important. If she had not abandoned the Townsend baby of her own free will, something sinister and puzzling must have happened...

Poor kid, Pollard thought, his mind starting off on another track. Immature, but just starting to feel the urgent need to have a life of her own, apart from her mother. A very vulnerable state, making her an easy prey to some plausible type with a diseased mind.

As he returned to the hotel, he reviewed the various enquiries he had set in motion. At Kittitoe, the movements of people and cars during the critical period on Friday night were being investigated. Here, at Stoneham, the local chaps were checking up on Wendy's friends. The anorak was being matched up with Ted Chugg's find at the forensic laboratory. All in order, but he had a sense of something overlooked. This lasted through a long soak in a hot bath, and it was not until he was getting into bed that he suddenly knew what it was. Why had Eddy Horner rung the school on Friday night? Had he any reason to suppose that Wendy either was or had been there? And if so, what was it?

At this point another idea struck him, and he collected the case file and hunted through it for Superintendent Crookshank's summary of developments up to the Yard's take-over. Yes, the telephone had been answered by Mrs Makepeace. There was no mention of one of the Horner staff being fetched, which implied that Eddy Horner was satisfied that she would have known if Wendy had shown up. And it was Mrs Makepeace whose quickwittedness had led to the discovery of the body. What was it that Crookshank said about her? 'Aged 28. Widow. Reliable type.' Quite a testimonial from a saturnine chap like that. Obviously she must be seen at once. There was nothing to stop her going off for the rest of the school holidays.

Cursing himself for not having thought about her as a potentially useful witness before, Pollard looked up St Julitta's telephone number in the case file and dialled it.

Leaning back on his pillows he annoyingly got the number engaged signal, replaced the receiver and waited. At the end of five minutes he tried again, with the same result. A third attempt was no more successful. Anyway, it looks as though she's still there, he thought. A caretaker would hardly go on nattering like this. I'll try first thing in the morning.

He had hardly put out his bedside light when his telephone bleeped.

'Stoneham Police Station, sir,' came a voice. 'There's just been a call for you from Kittitoe. A Mrs Marcia Makepeace of St Julitta's School would be glad if you could call to see her any time tomorrow. She has some information which she thinks might be of use to you.'

7

'Sir,' said Mr Pickwick, 'you're another.'
Pickwick Papers. Chapter 15

As they drove down to Kittitoe on the following morning, Pollard skimmed through the detailed information on
Eddy Horner and the two Townsends which the Yard had
amassed and sent to him. At intervals he read excerpts aloud
to Toye.

'Well, I hope that satisfies even your cautious mind,' he
said. 'A quite remarkable absence of skeletons in cupboards.'

It was a radiant morning. Pollard felt stimulated by having a definite objective in the shape of the interview asked
for by Mrs Makepeace. On arriving at Constable Pike's,
however, they were greeted by an unexpected development.
In the course of the house-to-house enquiry, Jack Nancekivell, landlord of the King William, had recognized Wendy
Shaw's photograph as that of a girl who had recently been
in his pub.

'Quick work, Pike,' Pollard complimented him. 'Let's go
right along.'

The King William's frontage on the village street was
modest, but its corner site and former stabling in the rear
had enabled it to expand to meet the increasing number of
visitors to the area. It was well-kept and had a welcoming
atmosphere, and Pollard could visualize it packed to suffoca-
tion during the holiday season. He wondered what there
could have been about Wendy Shaw to attract the landlord's
attention.

Jack Nancekivell was built foursquare, with a cheerful red face. Vigorous cleaning was in progress in the bars, and the three policemen were escorted into his private sanctum. Regretfully refusing offers of refreshment, Pollard put his question.

'Thought as you'd be askin' me that,' the landlord replied, 'seein' as you can't hardly lift yer elbow in 'ere summer evenins. At first glance she looked a proper kiddy, an' I sized 'er up careful, thinkin' she might be under age, before Joe served the chap she was with. Then I saw she was older than what I'd thought.'

'And what was the chap like, Mr Nancekivell?' Pollard asked hopefully.

'Ar, now y'r askin'. If only I'd known what was comin', but there. Tell the truth I didn't pay much 'eed to 'im. I wasn't servin' 'im, just keepin' me eye on things from t'other end of the bar, and the place was packed to bustin'. Young, an' shaggy like, same as most of 'em these days. Not tall or short, so as you'd notice.'

'Can you remember ever seeing him in here without the girl?'

'Lumme, sir! It ain't as though I ever 'ad 'im clear to start with. Maybe if I saw 'is photo, I'd call 'im to mind.'

Skilled questioning failed to elicit any further details of the young man's appearance, but Jack Nancekivell was confident that he had seen Wendy in the pub on one or two other occasions subsequently. Pressed for dates, he could only say that it had been within the past two or three weeks.

'Sorry I can't be no more 'elp,' he added.

'You've been quite a bit of help,' Pollard told him. 'It's possible we may ask you to come along to an identity parade one of these days. In the meantime, if you think of anything, or pick up anything when customers are talking in the bar, get on to me through Pike here, won't you?'

Five minutes later Toye brought the car to a standstill outside St Julitta's. The front door was open, and the sound of an electric polisher in use came from a room leading off the entrance hall. In response to a request for Mrs Makepeace, the woman who had been operating it escorted them up two flights of stairs, and along a passage to a door which was ajar. From within came a man's voice, expostulating angrily and excitedly. There was a sudden silence as their escort knocked loudly. The next moment the door was flung open by a tall, fair young woman with an expression of embarrassed annoyance. She swiftly converted this into one of polite greeting.

'Thank you for bringing these gentlemen up, Mrs Freen,' she said. 'Good morning. I'm Marcia Makepeace, and I take it you're Detective-Superintendent Pollard? Do come in, won't you?'

'Thank you,' Pollard replied, following her into the room. 'This is Inspector Toye, who is working with me on the case.' He looked pointedly at the man who stood with his back to the mantelpiece, flushed and frowning.

'Mr Medlicott, St Julitta's bursar,' Marcia Makepeace said rather hurriedly. 'Do sit down.'

Andrew Medlicott acknowledged Pollard's slight bow with a nod, murmured something about correspondence, and went quickly out of the room.

'There's such a lot to settle up after this course we've just had here,' Marcia Makepeace said, sitting down herself. 'It's good of you to come so soon. I expect you get a lot of tiresome people thinking they've something important to tell you, when it's really nothing at all.'

She sounded distraite and flustered, and Pollard gave her a breathing space by recapitulating the information in the file about Eddy Horner's telephone call to her on the previous Friday night, and the discovery of Wendy Shaw's body on Monday morning.

'Have I got all these points right, Mrs Makepeace?' he asked.

'Yes, absolutely.' She stopped as if uncertain how to go on.

'What I'd like you to do now, is to tell me about this course, and to what extent Mr Horner and the rest of his household were personally involved in it.'

At this she began to talk freely about the fire at the Horner hotel at Biddle Bay in the spring, Mr Horner's request to rent the school for the second and third weeks in August, and the general organization of the Fortnight. As he listened, Pollard unobtrusively took in the room and its contents.

70

Presumably it was her private sitting room, as it contained no office equipment. The studio portrait on the bureau of a young man with an attractive lively face was surely the dead husband—she was a widow, according to the file. His attention was sharpened by an unframed and unmounted photograph of a group of five people, three men and two women, also on the top of the bureau...

'That's roughly how the Fortnight ran,' Marcia Makepeace was saying. 'You asked if Mr Horner and his household were involved at all. The answer to that is not at all, except' —she hesitated fractionally—'that on the evening before it started he asked the lecturers, and myself, and Mr and Mrs Medlicott up to Uncharted Seas for drinks.'

'And this, I rather think, brings us to your reason for your asking me to come along this morning, doesn't it?'

Pollard smiled at her, but she did not respond.

'Well, I suppose it does—in a way.'

He waited, conscious of Toye in the background with his pen poised over his notebook. She had turned her face away, and was staring out of the window. Then, with a visible effort of will, she glanced quickly at him and began to speak. The words came slowly, as if carefully chosen.

'This drinks party was the first time I saw Wendy Shaw. She struck me as young and naïve, and—well—rather gauche. In the course of the evening she and one of our lecturers seemed to gravitate to each other to some extent. He was—is —a young man called Geoffrey Boothby.' Her eyes went involuntarily to the top of the bureau. 'I like him,' she went on with a touch of defiance. 'He's a bit way out. Untidy, long-haired, no social graces, apt to be aggressive, and so on. Immensely enthusiastic about the countryside, and geology, which is his shop. Very kind and patient to the Fortnighters, and I must say some of them were rather dim. Of course I don't believe for one single moment that he murdered Wendy Shaw,' she ended with rather a rush.

Pollard waited for a couple of moments.

'I think you've more than this to tell me, haven't you, Mrs Makepeace?' he asked. 'Did you see these two together on later occasions?'

'Only once. I saw them out together in Geoff Boothby's car.'

'That's still only twice you saw them together. Perhaps you've discussed it with someone else who had also seen them?'

To his surprise Marcia blushed, and then looked annoyed with herself.

'Surely you don't accept people's statements at second-hand?' she parried.

'Of course not. When you have given us this person's name, we shall check up.'

'Mr Michael Jay, who was in charge of the Fortnight, has told me that he saw Wendy and Geoff together in the bar of the King William once or twice,' she said, still slightly pink.

'When did Mr Jay leave here?' Pollard asked.

'Last Saturday morning.'

'And when did he give you this information?'

'Just before he went.'

'Was Mr Boothby here on Saturday morning?'

'Yes, he was.'

'In that case, then, there could have been no question of his having gone off with Wendy Shaw, could there? And on Saturday morning no one, except for her murderer, knew that she was dead. If I may say so, you don't strike me as a gossipy type, Mrs Makepeace. How did you and Mr Jay come to have this conversation on what must have been a very busy morning?'

'He knew Constable Pike had been round, and asked me if anything was up. I—I told him I was just a bit worried because I'd seen Geoff go out after the film show we had on Friday night. I didn't want to mention this to Pike, so I asked Mr Jay's advice.'

'Which was?' Pollard queried.

'That it wasn't in the least necessary. As you said, no one knew that Wendy had been killed at this stage.'

'And now that it is known, you decided that you ought to give us this information?'

'Well,—er, actually Mr Jay feels rather strongly that it ought to be passed on as things have turned out. He rang me about it yesterday morning, and again last night, when I'd had time to think it over. Last night,' she repeated, a shade absently, and then hurried on. 'He suggested contacting you himself, but we decided in the end that it would be simpler if I did, as anyway you'd want it firsthand in the end. Not that it means that either of us thinks that Geoff Boothby's involved in the very slightest. It's only that Mi—Mr Jay says that it's in Geoff's interests, and the police will find out, and so one might as well,' she ended rather incoherently.

'Mr Jay is a wise man,' Pollard said. 'We shall need to see him personally, of course. I take it you have his present address?'

He listened as Marcia explained that Michael Jay, the two Kings and Susan Crump were now conducting a Discovery Fortnight at Crowncliff on the south coast, but that Geoff Boothby, who was not a full-time member of the Horner staff, had returned to his home at Winnage on the previous Saturday. As far as she knew he was still there. She had the home address of all members of the Kittitoe Fortnight for forwarding correspondence.

Aware of a good many points which needed clearing up, Pollard looked at his watch and made a quick decision.

'Mrs Makepeace,' he said in a non-official tone, 'I hope this isn't sheer nerve on my part, but is there any chance of a cuppa? We made an awfully early start this morning.'

Marcia started to her feet with a horrified exclamation. 'How frightful of me, especially as I asked you to come! I do apologise. We'll have one at once—there's a pantry next door.'

As the door closed behind her Pollard swung round to Toye.

'Well?' he queried.

'That chap who was creating when we turned up looked a bit odd, I thought,' Toye commented. 'Nervy, and rattled.'

'Yea. And I got the impression that the dust-up they were having was something to do with our call. We'd better find out a bit more about Mr Medlicott. Anything else?'

'She's sweet on this bloke Jay.'

'Pretty quick work in a fortnight, what? Could it be that he was popping the question over the blower last night? The line down here was blocked long enough.'

'A very nice lady,' Toye said reprovingly. 'You wouldn't want her spending the rest of her life on her memories, would you?'

'Bless my soul! You must have started going to another sort of film. Come off romance, and keep your mind on the job.'

As he spoke Pollard got up and went across to the bureau. He picked up the unmounted photograph and studied it.

'I bet this is a group of the Horner staff who were here,' he said. 'The only one she's got of Jay. All the same we'll have to wrest it from her for a bit. It could be useful to get the young chap blown up. Possible lead, don't you think?'

Toye agreed.

'It's the first hint of anyone the Shaw girl went around with. Chances are he went out to the pub Friday night, the weather being what it was. Maybe Nancekivell'll recognize the photo.'

The door reopened, and he rose politely to relieve Marcia of the tray she was carrying.

In the more relaxed atmosphere over the cuppas Pollard managed to build up a clear picture of Geoff Boothby's exit on Friday night after the film show. Asked how she could be so definite about the time, Marcia explained that the evening was running late, owing to the delayed return from the expedition which had held up the final editing of the Fortnight film. She had counted on the entertainment being over by about nine-twenty, but it had gone on until ten minutes to ten, as an extra film had been put on first, while they waited for Mr King to finish the editing. This meant that the domestic staff on duty to serve tea and coffee after the film show were kept late, and she had been very clock conscious.

In reply to further questions, she had no idea when Geoff Boothby had returned. All five of the lecturers had been lent keys of the front door for the duration of the Fortnight. Mr Jay had told her that when he went up to his room at ten minutes past twelve, there had been no light in Geoff Boothby's, next door to him, and he had assumed that the latter had already turned in. At all events he had not heard anyone come in later.

'Thank you,' Pollard said. 'I've got all that quite clear.

Speaking of the lecturers, I've been noticing that recent-looking unframed photograph on your bureau. Does Mr Boothby feature in it?'

'Yes, he does,' Marcia admitted unwillingly. 'Mr King, who's almost a professional, took a lot of groups of members of the Fortnight, and people bought them as souvenirs.'

'I'm going to ask you to lend us that one of yours for a short time, then. Great care will be taken of it, and we'll give you a receipt. Don't look so distressed, Mrs Makepeace. Let's face it. If Mr Boothby has nothing to do with Wendy Shaw's death, the sooner we clear up his movements on Friday night, the better for him. If he has, well, I don't think you'd want to shield him, would you?'

Without replying, she got up and fetched the photograph for him.

'Thank you,' Pollard said. 'The young chap with long hair and sideburns is Boothby, I take it? Make out a receipt, will you, Inspector? Now just one last point. Was Mr Medlicott at the film show?'

Marcia looked surprised.

'Not that I know of. He's a bird watcher, so I suppose he might have been invited down to see the extra film on birds that was shown first. I believe he went on one of Paul King's expeditions. But I didn't see him around, and he certainly didn't come in for tea afterwards.'

On the way out Pollard and Toye waited while she fetched the list of addresses from her office.

'I thought you might like to have the whole lot,' she said, handing him some sheets of typescript fastened together.

'How very efficient,' Pollard commented. 'Even the car registration numbers.'

'Absolutely essential, the way people park. There always seemed to be somebody being asked to move.'

He put the lists into his briefcase, and asked her when she planned to leave Kittitoe.

'I had meant to go today, actually. But with all this upset we're behindhand with the cleaning. Is there any reason—I mean, do you want me to stay around?'

'I shouldn't feel justified in asking you to do that. Are you by any chance going abroad for the rest of the holidays?'

'Oh, no. I shall be in London. I can give you my address there.'

'That's all I want, just to be able to contact you if necessary. Perhaps you'd let Pike know when you decide to go?'

'Certainly I will. Here's the address.'

'Thank you for being so helpful, Mrs Makepeace. I can only say that I'm very sorry you've been involved in all this.'

A few minutes later they drove away from the school.

By now trade was brisk in the bars of the King William, but Jack Nancekivell obligingly extricated himself. Asked if he recognized anyone in the photograph of the five Horner lecturers, he studied it with knotted brow.

'I've seen all this lot in 'ere, the last week or two,' he said, 'but it's the young chap you're after, isn't it? Well, 'e came in Friday night, an' 'ad words with Mr Bleeding Snooper Stubbs. Didn't come to nothin', but I 'ad me eye on 'em.'

'What time was this?' Pollard asked.

'Just gone twenty after ten. 'E come in, with Stubbs right on 'is 'eels, an' started shovin' 'is way up to the bar. Stubbs got 'old of 'is arm, an' started 'oldin' forth, but the young chap shook 'im orf, an' came on up, an' arst for a double whisky. No, 'e wasn't sozzled, but 'e looked properly browned orf. Gulped down 'is whisky, an' pushed out again. But this ain't what you're after.' Pausing, the landlord subjected the photograph to another lengthy stare. 'No, t'ain't no bloomin' good,' he said at last. "E's like the chap the Shaw girl was with, but I couldn't swear to it. Not on my bible oath, I couldn't. Sorry.'

'OK,' Pollard said. 'Who's this Mr Stubbs you don't seem to be all that keen on?'

Jack Nancekivell's reply was colourful. Pollard gathered that Mr Stubbs was against visitors, and anybody in Kittitoe who tried to make an honest living out of them. He wanted the village kept for what he called the residents, and this mostly meant chaps like himself, not Kittitoe born at all, but who'd retired there for the cheap living. What he expected people to live on who hadn't retired on pensions or had private fortunes was anybody's guess. Stubbs and Don Glover who'd started up the caravan site were daggers drawn. Almost came to blows right here in the bar they did, last spring...

With some difficulty Pollard stemmed a complex narrative involving visits to the village by a fish and chips van, the illuminated sign at the entrance to the caravan site, and the enlargement of the public convenience. In reply to a direct question, Jack Nancekivell said that he'd sign a statement about the young chap in the photo and Stubbs, so long as it put things proper. Where did Stubbs live? Along the street, and second on the left, in an old place he'd bought cheap and had done up. All la-di-da and tubs of flowers round it... Wouldn't the two gentlemen like a bit of lunch? They didn't do lunches, not as a rule, but the wife always had a ham on the go, and there was nothing wrong with King William beer —folk came in for it from miles round.

By now Pollard and Toye were decidedly hungry, and accepted the offer with alacrity. Mrs Nancekivell's idea of a bite was comprehensive, and they left the pub half an hour later feeling comfortably replete.

There was no difficulty in locating Mr Stubbs's house from the landlord's description. External decoration and surrounding garden were in a state of unnatural perfection, suggesting a photograph in a glossy magazine. Pollard pressed a bell push, and a decorous burr sounded within.

The door was opened by a grey-haired man immaculate in light suit, collar and tie. He scrutinized the callers through rimless spectacles, contriving to give the impression of having been summoned from work of importance. Accepting Pollard's official card, he examined it carefully.

'Ah, yes,' he said, in a voice lacking both volume and resonance. 'Detective-Superintendent Pollard. I have been anticipating a call from you. Come in. We shall not be disturbed in my study.'

As they followed, Pollard risked a wink at Toye. The study was a small, austerely furnished room, with a huge kneehole desk on which stood a typewriter and several wire baskets of correspondence. There was also a filing cabinet, and a bookcase containing standard reference books and numerous pamphlets. One wall was almost completely covered by an enormous large-scale map of the village and its environs. Mr Stubbs seated himself at the desk, and indicated two chairs facing it.

'And in what way, Superintendent,' he enquired, clasping his hands and resting them on a silver-mounted blotter, 'can I be of assistance to you in your enquiry? No doubt Superintendent Bostock of Winnage has already shown you my letter?'

'Quite,' replied Pollard, rallying swiftly to this unexpected development. 'But I'm sure you'll understand that we always find it helpful to go over the ground again at first hand.'

'A very proper attitude, if I may say so. I shall endeavour to give you a full and accurate account of the incident dealt with in my letter, beginning with my departure from this house at approximately 9.45 on the night of last Friday.'

Mr Stubbs broke off, and glanced at Toye, who had taken out his notebook. Apparently satisfied that a record was to be made of his utterances, he adopted the relaxed position of a man about to expound at length.

'On Friday evening last,' he began, 'my wife and I had supper at eight, as is our custom during the summer months. After the meal had been eaten and cleared away, I read *The Times,* and watched the nine o'clock news on BBC 1. As the following programme was wholly trivial, and held no interest for me, I finished my perusal of *The Times*. At a quarter to ten precisely I set out to give our spaniel his final run of the day.'

'You must be a devoted dog owner,' Pollard interposed. 'I understand that it was an appalling evening.'

'You understand correctly, Superintendent. It was raining heavily, and a strong southerly wind was blowing. For this reason I took Humphrey in my car, going through the village and out on to the Biddle Bay road. Here I drew up, and let Humphrey out for a run in the dunes. I turned the car, allowed him about ten minutes, and then we started back. I need not say that I was driving with special care owing to the heavy rain and poor visibility. As I reached the drive entrance to Uncharted Seas, the residence of Mr Edward Horner, a car suddenly shot out at high speed, positively forcing me into the nearside hedge. It tore on, and I could see its lights disappearing into the car park of the King William inn. I followed, determined to remonstrate with the driver. When I got to the car park myself, a young man was coming

78

away from the vehicle in question, one of these noisy dangerous sports car which are responsible for so many of our road accidents. I called out to him, and he ignored me. I followed him into the inn, and attempted to speak to him. He merely uttered an obscene expression and made for the bar. Rather than create a disturbance, I left the premises, and took the number of his car. I then returned home, and wrote a strong letter of complaint to Superintendent Bostock of Winnage, to which, I may say, I have not yet received the courtesy of a reply.'

'May Inspector Toye have a copy of this letter for a moment? No doubt you kept a carbon, Mr Stubbs?'

'Certainly. It is my invariable practice. I have it filed here.'

Going across to the filing cabinet, Mr Stubbs swiftly extracted the letter, and handed it over with an air of being gratified by his own efficiency.

'I did not realize at the time,' he added, 'how important this step I had taken might prove to be.'

'Did you recognize the car?' Pollard asked.

'I did not. It was the noisy dangerous type one associates with the highly irresponsible young men of the present day.'

'Do you recognize anyone in this photograph?'

Mr Stubbs took one look at the group of the five lecturers, and without the slightest hesitation indicated Geoff Boothby.

'This is the young man who nearly crashed into me on Friday evening, and was offensively rude in the King William afterwards. I am prepared to state this on oath. I congratulate you, Superintendent, on running him to earth so promptly. It will not surprise me in the very least to learn that he has been charged with that young woman's murder.'

'No charge is being preferred against this young man at the moment,' Pollard replied. 'Why didn't you report the near accident to Constable Pike?'

Mr Stubbs assumed a long-suffering expression.

'It shall suffice to say, Superintendent, that on previous occasions I have found Pike unco-operative over matters of dangerous driving and undesirable behaviour by visitors. Consequently, I now appeal to Caesar.'

Caesar be blowed, Pollard thought. Of course, the letter

went into a non-urgent file at the Winnage station, its real importance being overlooked...

He realized that a further grievance was being aired.

'...still less hope of getting the second complaint in my letter dealt with by Pike. I had another narrow escape from a serious motor accident on Friday night. As I edged out of the car park at the inn—with the greatest care, on account of the poor visibility—a Mr Glover, resident in the village, came down the street in his car at quite sixty miles an hour. Had I not been able to stop dead, he would have gone straight into me. There was not the smallest...'

'Which direction was he coming from?' interrupted Pollard.

'From the Winnage direction, going towards Biddle Bay.'

'Are you prepared to swear that this second car was being driven by Mr Glover?'

'Under the circumstances it was hardly practicable to read the number plate, or positively to identify the driver,' Mr Stubbs replied huffily. 'The car was all too familiar. Mr Glover owns a white Ford Capri, and the outrageous driving was typical of him. As President of the Kittitoe Residents' Association I have made endless complaints in the interests of public safety...'

The tirade continued in a slightly rising key, accompanied by thumps on the desk with a clenched fist. Observing Mr Stubbs with interest, Pollard noticed a certain weakness about his chin.

When they had extricated themselves, and regained their car, he turned to Toye.

'Anything strike you in all this tub thumping?' he asked.

'Sounds as though there was quite a crowd around at the Horner bungalow end of the village on Friday night, say between ten and half-past, doesn't it?'

'Yea. However, let's get down to brass tacks, and compare this car number Stubbs gave us with Boothby's on Mrs Make-peace's list.'

Investigation showed that the numbers were identical. Toye whistled briefly.

'Don't start chucking your hat in the air,' Pollard said. 'Have you thought about the time factor? If Boothby didn't leave the school premises until ten minutes to ten, when the film show ended, and Nancekivell saw him come into the pub at twenty past or a minute or two later, it's damnably tight, you know. How long would it take to drive up to Uncharted Seas?'

'For a young chap who blinds along? Four minutes, door to door? Same coming down, I'd say.'

'That gives him about twenty minutes up there to commit the murder, get the body into Beckon Cove, and collect the handbag, unless the girl brought it out of the bungalow with her. Possible, I suppose, but we're still left with the problem of where the murder was actually committed. Incidentally, Stubbs was out and about five minutes earlier, wasn't he?'

Toye looked incredulous.

'You don't seriously think that old geyser?—'

Pollard grinned.

'You can't have been reading the papers lately. Endless articles about the sexual potentiality of the elderly. No, but seriously, I'm not washing out Stubbs altogether. The man's a fanatic. Did you see his eyes as he ranted and banged the desk? And the slope of his chin? Over-compensation, and what-have-you. I wonder if there's any means of checking what time he went out? Let's go and pump Pike.'

A few minutes later Toye drew up behind a badly-parked white Ford Capri at the gate of the police house. They looked at each other. As he switched off the engine, sounds of an altercation came from an open window.

'We seem to be making a habit of turning up at awkward moments,' Pollard remarked. 'We'll gatecrash this time.'

As they went quietly up to the door, the owner of a broad back in a sports shirt was objecting forcibly to police enquiries at his caravan site.

'...enough to make the whole damn crowd pack up and clear out. Who wants coppers mucking around when they've come for a holiday?'

'Who indeed?' agreed Pollard, neatly fielding the ball as he walked in. 'Who is this gentleman, Constable?'

There was a startled silence. Pike, standing behind his desk, came smartly to attention.

'This is Mr Glover, sir, the owner of the Kittitoe Caravan Site. He wishes to lodge a complaint about his tenants being questioned about their movements last Friday night.'

'Good afternoon, Mr Glover. I am Detective-Superintendent Pollard of New Scotland Yard, in charge of the investigation into the murder of Miss Wendy Shaw. In this connection, every house in the area is being visited, and the inmates asked if they can give any information. What exactly is your complaint?'

The man standing with his back to the window was burly, with a square suntanned face, and bright watchful eyes. Pollard recognized an underlying uneasiness, and a quick decision to compound for civility.

'I'm not complaining about the enquiry. Whoever killed the girl's got to be run to earth. But there's no call to set the whole place by the ears. If Pike here had come to me first, I'd have put him on to the site manager, and the whole business could have been done without upsetting people.'

'There's no occasion for innocent people to be upset by being asked a few questions, Mr Glover. My experience is that members of the public enjoy the experience—unless they have anything to hide, of course. Incidentally, I was going to call on you yourself this afternoon with a question. When you drove through the village in the direction of Biddle Bay, at about ten-twenty-five last Friday night, did you notice any person or any vehicle near the drive entrance to Mr Horner's bungalow?'

There was an electric silence, in the course of which Don Glover swallowed, and moistened his lips.

'I remember a car coming out of the pub car park,' he replied off-handedly. 'Nothing else. It was a lousy night—raining like hell.'

Pollard glanced at Toye.

'Take this down, Inspector,' he said. 'We'll get a statement typed out for you later, Mr Glover, and ask you to read it over and sign it.'

Don Glover leant back against the window sill, his posture over-emphasizing relaxation.

'What time was it when you drove back into Kittitoe?' Pollard asked.

'Say five minutes later.'

There was an interrogative silence.

'Damn it!' Don Glover finally burst out. 'Why should I have to give an account of my private affairs like this? If you must know, I'd started out for Biddle to see a chap on business, and my windscreen wiper suddenly packed up. No one but a bloody fool would have tried to carry on.'

'Very wise of you to turn back, Mr Glover. I wish all motorists were as cautious. Did you see anyone about this time?'

'Not a soul.'

'Do you live in the village?'

'Half a mile out on the Winnage road.'

'And what time did you get home from this abortive trip to Biddle Bay?'

'God, I don't know to the minute. Why should I? About quarter to eleven, I suppose.'

'Would any member of your household have noticed?'

'My wife might. Nobody else was in. Why not ask her? Or isn't a wife's evidence worth having?'

'Well, thank you, Mr Glover,' Pollard replied, ignoring this final remark. 'We needn't keep you any longer now. I hope your tenants will settle down again. Tiresome about your windscreen wiper. Have you been able to get a replacement yet?'

'Fixed it myself,' Don Glover said briefly.

With a curt nod he strode out of the room. A minute later the Capri roared into life, gave a bucketing leap and shot off.

'Worth a week's pay, that was,' Pike remarked unexpectedly, and promptly reddened at having spoken out of turn.

Pollard sat down astride an upright chair, clasping the back with both hands.

'Tell us all about the bellicose but rattled Mr Glover,' he said.

He listened with keen interest to an account of numerous and financially successful business enterprises, and determined attempts to climb the social ladder.

'A governor of St Julitta's?' he exclaimed in some surprise.

'That's right, sir. They've had a lot of building done up there, and he's had the contract most times. Mind you, his work's good, and I reckon he's often been a help to them with advice over the place. I'd say that's how they came to take his daughter as a day scholar. They only have a few of those—just the local gentry. Then he gave a big sum to their appeal fund, and, well, they more or less had to have him on the board, by the look of it.'

'What do you suppose he was up to on Friday night?' Pollard asked. 'Could it be a bird over at Biddle Bay?'

Pike scratched his head.

'I wouldn't think so, sir. Very devoted couple, Mr and Mrs Glover, for all that she's a quiet little mouse of a woman. He'd go blasting around twice as much again if it weren't for her. I can't figure out what he was so het up about. That yarn about his windscreen wiper didn't ring true, not to me, it didn't. He's that reckless on the road I don't see him turning back for a thing like that.'

Pollard considered.

'If you'll excuse me, sir, there's a report I'd like to make. I called on a Mrs Coates this morning. Her husband's a bank manager in Winnage : very reliable couple, they are, living next to the Vicarage. They went over to Biddle Bay last Friday night, to dinner with some friends, and were driving back into the village just on half-past eleven. They saw a man come out of either the drive entrance to the school, or Mr Horner's, but were too far away to say which. Then the man started walking in their direction, and when they got close, they saw it was Mr Medlicott, the gentleman that does the accounts at the school. He lives in one of the new bungalows out on the Biddle road.'

Pollard raised his eyebrows, and looked at Toye.

'Surprisingly popular, that end of the village last Friday night, from the look of things. It's time we put you in the picture, Pike.'

He summarized their visit to St Julitta's, the finding of the strip of scarlet cloth in Beckon Cove, the coastguard's opinion on the disposal of Wendy Shaw's body, and the evidence of Jack Nancekivell and Mr Stubbs.

'You must be thankful that Mr Stubbs goes over your head with his complaints against all and sundry,' Pollard concluded. 'How does Winnage take it?'

'They soon got him sized up, sir, after he'd been in to see

the Super once or twice. They just pass whatever it is on to me, and if it's anything to take up, I make enquiries, and report back.'

'Is there a Mrs Stubbs?'

'Why, yes, sir, and some holds she's worse than he is about what they call conserving the village. She drives folk up the wall at the WI, my wife says.'

'Who else is there in the household?'

'There's only the two of them. Their son's gone to live in Australia.'

'Wise man, from the sound of it. So it's not going to be all that easy to get satisfactory confirmation of the time Stubbs started out on Friday night, is it? You see how my mind's working, Pike? What's your reaction to the possibility of him being involved in the murder?'

Rather to Pollard's surprise, Pike showed no astonishment, but considered the question carefully for several seconds.

'I wouldn't rule it out right away, sir,' he replied cautiously, scratching his head again, and frowning heavily. 'Mind you, I've no reason to think he's a violent man, but you wouldn't believe the state he gets into over litter, say, or a bit o' rowdiness, holiday times. Proper steamed up and all of a sweat. And if he comes on a young couple having a go, you'd think the world was coming to an end, the way he carries on. I reckon he's a bit of a Peeping Tom. If I was Chairman up at the school in Mr Cary's place, I'd a lot rather have Mr Glover on the board than Mr Stubbs, for all that he's for ever shooting off his mouth.'

'How many more possible suspects are connected with that school, do you think?' Pollard asked Toye. 'The best thing that could happen from my point of view would be for my aunt to have been seen hanging around on Friday night. Then I could ask to be relieved of the blasted case!'

8

It shall be what o'clock I say it is.
            The Taming of the Shrew.
                        Act 4 Scene i

On their way to Winnage to interview Geoff Boothby,
Pollard and Toye turned down a minor road and parked in a
gateway. Here they drew up a timetable for the night of
Wendy Shaw's murder, at first working independently as
their habit was, and finally pooling results. Using the back
of his briefcase as a writing desk, Pollard made a fair copy.

'How's that?' He handed it over to Toye, who propped it
on the steering wheel, and instantly became immersed.

Unemployed for the moment, Pollard got out of the car
and rested his arms along the topmost bar of the gate. The
field inside had been down to oats, already harvested and
carried. The stubble was laced with vivid green weeds, and
starred here and there with the scarlet of persistent poppies.
After an overcast morning the sun had broken through, and
soft white clouds moved slowly over a pale blue sky. There
was a tang of autumn in the air, and from far above filaments
of lark song drifted down, treble to the steady bass of a
combine crawling over a neighbouring field. Pollard let out
a contented sigh, letting it all wash over him. At a movement in the car behind him he turned reluctantly.

'Nothing left out that I can see,' Toye said.

Pollard got in and sat beside him. With the timetable
between them, they lit cigarettes.

86

FRIDAY AUGUST 20th
PM

7.00	Horner and daughter leave by car for Stoneham.
8.00	Wendy Shaw takes a telephone call: caller Aunt Is.
9.45	Stubbs claims to have started out in car.
9.50	Film show ends at St J's. Boothby goes out.
10.15 approx.	Horner rings Uncharted Seas from Stoneham, and gets no answer. Stubbs claims Boothby's car comes out of UC's drive.
10.20 approx.	Boothby enters bar of King William, followed by Stubbs.
10.25 approx.	Stubbs says Glover drove past pub heading for Biddle Bay Road. Glover confirms this.
10.30 approx.	Boothby leaves pub.
10.45	Glover thinks he arrived home.
11.30 approx.	Coates see Medlicott coming out of either Horner's or St J's drive.
11.40	Horner and Townsends return to bungalow.
11.55	Horner rings Mrs Makepeace.

SATURDAY AUGUST 21st
AM

12.10 approx.	Michael Jay goes up to bed.

QUERIES
(1) Did Stubbs actually leave home earlier?
(2) Was he parked alongside the Biddle Bay road from the time he arrived until a few minutes before 10.15, as he claims?
(3) Where did Boothby go when he came out of the pub?
(4) Where was Glover between 10.25 pm and his return home?
(5) Where was Medlicott coming from at 11.30 pm?

'At the moment,' Pollard said, after a pause, 'we've got to leave these queries for Pike and Co to work on. Let's try a different approach. I'll think up a case against each of these blokes, and you try to knock it down. Our usual roles, in

fact. Here goes with Boothby. On your reckoning, and allow-
ing, say, a couple of minutes for getting away after the film
show, he could have got up to Uncharted Seas several
minutes before ten. Fifteen minutes to strangle the girl, heave
the body over into Beckon Cove, collect the handbag, and
have a near miss with Stubb's car by 10.15. Tight, but just
possible.'

'Barely,' Toye objected. 'Doesn't it assume she had her coat
and bag all ready to go out with him, which doesn't tie up
with the sort of girl she seems to have been. And could he
have got clear of the school in two minutes?'

'Assume objections granted, then. Did he pay a return visit
after having a stiffener at the pub, and get rid of the body
then? Or even do the job then?'

Toye gave this suggestion careful consideration, referring
to the timetable.

'It's possible on paper. Glover said he didn't see anybody
on his return trip, and they could easily have missed. Boothby
may have sat in his car for a bit.'

'Yes, they could. And the fact remains that Boothby's
known to have been in touch with Wendy, while we don't
so far know that of any of these other chaps. Let's go on to
Stubbs. See Queries (1) and (2). Surely this dog-exercising on
a pouring wet night's a bit thin, especially for anyone getting
on a bit?'

Toye was doubtful. It was staggering what people would
do for their dogs. Give him a cat any day. Leads its own
life, and doesn't thank you for butting in.

'We'll give him the benefit of the doubt, then. But there's
Pike's opinion of him, which is interesting. I'd say there were
some hefty repressions there, wouldn't you, and sex could
quite well come into it. On the other hand, there's no evidence so far that he'd ever met Wendy. If not, and he went up
to the bungalow for some other reason, what was it?'

'Might have wanted to see Horner about litter, or something. Could he have come on Boothby and Wendy Shaw
going the pace in the sand dunes sometime, or in Boothby's
car? That would've knocked him for six, according to Pike.'

'You're getting quite imaginative,' Pollard remarked. 'It's
an idea. But if it was Boothby and Wendy, it must have hap-

pened on Thursday, at least, because of that expedition on the Friday, and I can't see Stubbs waiting all that time to break the news to Horner. If it was just litter, or something of that sort, wouldn't he have rung Horner? Perhaps not. You can be choked off more easily on the blower. Make a note to ask Horner if he had any dealings with Stubbs, though.'

Toye made a careful entry in his notebook.

'Now for Glover,' Pollard resumed. 'It's just struck me that we don't know what time he started out on the trip through the village, or how he spent the earlier part of the evening, say from eight onwards. What do you think about Glover having committed the murder earlier, and gone back to dump the body in Beckon Cove? Not much, do you? Your face is an open book.'

'This going back idea doesn't make sense to me, sir. Much too risky.'

'You know, I think Boothby might have killed her on impulse, panicked and then pulled himself together and made a move to save his skin after his double whiskey. I agree the idea doesn't tick where Glover's concerned. And if he'd done the whole job earlier on, I don't see him revisiting the neighbourhood so soon. But all the same, what was he doing over there? That story about a trip to see a chap on business and the windscreen wiper just stinks. We'd better look into where he was from eight o'clock onwards.'

Toye made a further note.

'Finally, Medlicott, the chap who wasn't at all pleased to see us this morning. According to Mrs Makepeace, even if he was at the film show, he didn't stay on for the eats afterwards. So why was he coming away from the school as late as eleven-thirty?'

'Meaning he was more likely to be coming away from Horner's?' Toye asked. 'Mightn't there have been quite a lot of bookwork to do as the Fortnight affair was winding up the next day?'

'So pressing that it couldn't wait till the next morning? And if he went to work in his office, it seems odd that Mrs Makepeace didn't know about it. I'm sure she would have mentioned it when his name came up this morning. But of course, he might simply have gone over to St J's to fetch a book or something. Here again, there's no known contact with Wendy Shaw. Boothby's much the most likely candidate, isn't he? I suppose we'd better push along and see him...'

Toye turned the car, and edged out on to the main Kittitoe-Winnage road. Pollard was silent for some miles, having suddenly been seized with qualms at not having contacted the Winnage police as soon as Boothby had been mentioned by Marcia Makepeace. Perhaps it had been a mistake to wait until Nancekivell and Stubbs had seen the photograph. Suppose the chap had done a bunk? On the other hand, one mustn't go into an interview with the outcome prejudged...It was a relief to learn on arrival at the police station that Boothby was at his parents' home, with the engine of his car partly dismantled.

Over cups of tea Superintendent Bostock provided some background information. The Boothbys were highly respectable, and quite comfortably off. Mr Boothby Senior was the Town Architect, and Mrs Boothby a leading light in local good works. The son had gone to Winnage Grammar School, and won a scholarship to Birmingham University. He was now a teacher at Warhampton Comprehensive. There was nothing against him locally, except a minor motoring offence a few years back. No drugs, or getting mixed up with cranks. He'd had one or two girl friends, but nothing had come of it. He seemed more interested in cars than girls. Went to rallies, and so on.

'Thanks very much,' Pollard said. 'All that's very useful when it comes to tackling him. If he won't play at all, we may bring him along here, and put him through it. We may want to play it cool at this stage, but have an eye kept on him. Could you fix that?'

Superintendent Bostock thought this could be managed.

The Boothbys lived in a moderate-sized modern house, standing in a well-kept garden. A short drive curved round to the front door, sending a branch to a double garage. A sports car had been backed out of this, and a pair of legs in grimy blue jeans were protruding from the driver's seat.

'Triumph Two,' Toye muttered. 'Quite a nice job.'

As he approached with Pollard, the legs became animated, and the owner's body rose into view. A young man somewhere in his middle twenties confronted them. Mentally divesting him of a good deal of untidy light brown hair, Pollard registered a good brow and a pair of intelligent hazel eyes. In these a quick surmise was replaced by defensiveness.

'Mr Geoffrey Boothby?' Pollard asked.

The young man nodded without speaking.

Pollard introduced Toye and himself with the usual formula.

'We are conducting the enquiry into the murder of Miss Wendy Shaw,' he added, 'and think you may be able to help us with some information.'

Geoff Boothby remained poker-faced.

'Better come inside,' he said gruffly. 'Everybody's out.'

He put down the spanner he was holding, and led the way into the house, and what appeared to be the family sitting room. The exaggerated contrast with that of the Shaw family flashed through Pollard's mind. Here was freshness and colour, comfort, flowers, photographs, and a litter of people's belongings: books and periodicals, a chessboard with a game in progress, some knitting and a dog basket with a rubber bone in it. A large television set occupied one corner. It struck Pollard that grubby and unkempt though he looked, Geoff Boothby seemed perfectly at home in this setting. Not all that way out, he thought, and going to play it dumb.

'Mr Boothby,' he opened, 'I propose to ask you some questions about your movements last Friday night. It is my duty to tell you that you are entitled to have a solicitor present if you wish to send for one.'

Geoff Boothby flung himself back in his chair, his arms behind his head.

'No thanks,' he replied.

'Very well. It's entirely up to you. When did you first meet Wendy Shaw?'

The question was unexpected. The young man wrinkled his brow for a moment.

'Sixth of August,' he said.

'Where was this meeting?'

'At old Horner's place at Kittitoe.'

'How did you both come to be there?'

'Wendy was working for Horner's daughter. He'd asked the staff of the Fortnight up to drinks the night before it started.'

'Was anyone else present?'

'Mrs Makepeace, the school housekeeper. The chap who does the accounts for them, and his wife. Another man came in later. Glover, I think the name was.'

Pollard sensed Toye's interest.

'Did you see much of Wendy Shaw at this party?'

'Depends what you mean by much.'

'Let's put it another way, then. Did this first meeting lead to others?'

Geoff Boothby stared at his dirty canvas shoes.

'We met again, yes.'

Laboriously Pollard extracted admissions to outings in the car, and a couple of drinks at the King William.

'Why did Wendy tell Mr Horner and Mrs Townsend that she was going out with a girl friend from home?' he asked.

'Because of her mother.'

'OK,' Pollard said, 'I've met Mrs Shaw.'

For the first time Geoff Boothby showed signs of recognizing him as a human being. Their eyes met.

'Enough said, then.'

'Perhaps I'd better fill in,' Pollard replied. 'Stop me if you don't agree. Mrs Shaw, for reasons connected with her past life, was abnormally demanding and possessive towards Wendy, who had so far found it impossible to break away. Am I right?'

'If you can call an understatement like that right. The woman's a bloody vampire. Wendy hadn't even begun to live...'

'I suggest,' Pollard went on, 'that almost from your first meeting with Wendy, you tried to persuade her to make a break with her mother and start having a life of her own.'

'All right,' Geoff Boothby muttered, after a pause. 'If you must know, I wanted to marry her.'

'Did she agree to this?'

'No. The bitch of a mother had conditioned her into thinking she'd got to stick with her.'

'When was the last time you saw Wendy, Mr Boothby?'

'Thursday evening. The night before she—she died.'

By further questions Pollard elicited the information that Wendy had refused to meet again, but Geoff had announced that he was coming up to see her on the following evening, when she would be alone. She had replied that she would not let him in.

'To save time,' Pollard said, 'we have proof that you did go up to the bungalow, at about ten o'clock. Did you see Wendy? This isn't a trap: the police are not allowed to make false statements when questioning people.'

'No, I didn't see her. I can't prove it, of course. Are you going to arrest me?'

'If I were, I should have cautioned you. What I want from you now is a detailed statement of how you spent Friday evening, say from six onwards.'

He listened to a series of disjointed statements on the late return from Starbury Bay due to a misunderstanding with the coach drivers, the special last-night dinner, the hold-up over the Fortnight film while Paul King finished editing the last part, and the showing of one of his bird films while the audience waited. Because of this, the show had dragged on until ten minutes to ten.

'Are you sure of the time here?' he asked.

'My God, yes. I thought the damn thing was never going to end.'

'Why didn't you slip out?'

'There'd already been remarks about my cutting evening fixtures by some of my colleagues.'

'How long did it take you to get clear of the school building and drive up to Uncharted Seas?'

Geoff Boothby changed his position impatiently.

'Hell, I don't know to the minute! How should I? I waited until a few chaps had slunk off to the pub as soon as the show ended. Then I followed on, but found I couldn't get my car out.'

'Out of where?' Pollard asked, trying to keep the keen interest out of his voice.

'Where I'd parked her. Mike Jay, the OC of the Fortnight, had reserved a place for staff between the front porch and where the first big bay of the front sticks out on the right.

There was just room for three. I was up against the side of the bay, if you follow, and some clot had parked in front of the bay, and overlapping me a bit.'

'What did you do?'

'I had a couple of shots at getting out. The second time I just touched Mike. Then I tried to shift his car, but he'd locked it. So had the chap who was blocking me, but the passenger window wasn't quite up, and after a bit I managed to get it down enough to put my arm in and take the brake off.'

'Surely it would have been much quicker to go in and find either Mr Jay or the owner of the car?'

'Couldn't stand the thought of the jabbering crowd and the fuss.'

'Go on, then.'

'Well, I got out at last, and streaked up to the bungalow.' Pollard paused deliberately.

'Now, I want you to take your time before you answer this, Mr Boothby. How long do you estimate that it took you to get there from the ending of the film show at ten minutes to ten?'

In the silence which followed he was conscious of Toye's pen expectantly poised over his notebook, of the smooth ticking of a carriage clock on the mantelpiece, and of the tiny impact of a rose petal dropping on to a table.

'Fifteen minutes, near enough,' Geoff Boothby announced suddenly.

'What did you do when you arrived?'

'Rang the bell. Several times.'

'Did you try the door?'

'Yes. It was locked.'

'And then?'

'I lifted the flap of the letter box, and looked in.'

'Did you see or hear anything of Wendy Shaw?'

'No. At least, I could hear the telly in the lounge, so I thought she was in there.'

'Did you call to her?'

'Yes.'

'But there was no answer?'

'None.'

'Did you do anything else to attract her attention?'

94

'I hammered on the door.'

'I put it to you,' Pollard said slowly and deliberately, 'that you then went round to the garden door on the west side of the bungalow, found it unlocked, and went into the inside, and along the passage to the lounge.'

'And found Wendy there, and strangled her? Go on, why don't you say it?'

'They're your words, not mine, Mr Boothby. You deny having got into the bungalow by any means?'

'Absolutely. Try to prove it.'

'We try to get at the facts, not to establish unsupported possibilities. What did you do next, then, if you didn't gain entry to the bungalow?'

'I cleared off. I could see it was no go. I thought I'd go to the pub.'

'Did you meet anyone on the way there?'

'I was coming out of the drive a bit fast, and just missed a chap on the port side. He followed me into the pub and started bellyaching, but I shook him off. I had a drink. Didn't notice any of the Fortnight people, though.'

'And then?'

'I went back to the school.'

'Did anyone see you come in?'

'I don't think so. I slipped into the library, and sat in the dark a bit. I wanted to think things out, and it wasn't likely anyone would butt in.'

'How long were you there?' Pollard persevered.

For the first time Geoff Boothby seemed ill at ease, and hesitated.

'I wasn't tight, so I suppose you'll think I'm nuts, or am making it up. I didn't stay long, because I felt I was being watched.'

Pollard looked at him sharply.

'Do you mean you thought someone you couldn't see was also in the library?'

'Dunno what I thought. Only that it got under my skin, and I pushed off to bed after about ten minutes. Somehow I wasn't keen on switching on the lights.'

'Someone must have noticed you going upstairs, surely?'

'There wasn't anyone around as far as I remember. Thin, isn't it?'

Without replying, Pollard sat thinking.

'When does your term begin?' he asked at last.

'Seventh of September.'

'If you leave here before then, please notify Superintendent Bostock of your address. And I must ask you for your passport, please.'

The word 'fantastic' floated back as Geoff Boothby left the room. Through the open door came the sound of footsteps going upstairs. Pollard and Toye exchanged glances. There was a distant opening and shutting of drawers, and the footsteps began to return.

Accepting the passport held out to him without comment, Pollard checked it and put it into his briefcase.

'Anything you want to ask Mr Boothby before we go, Inspector?' he asked, turning to Toye.

'Did you happen to notice the make of the car that was blocking your exit, sir?'

'Good Lord, yes. Cars are my thing. An Austin 1100.'

As they glanced back on reaching the drive gate, he was standing by his car with bent head, absently kicking the offside rear tyre.

'No,' Pollard said in reply to Toye's unspoken question, 'I don't think he did it. Whether we can get confirmation of that hold-up over getting away after the film show is another matter, though. Also that he really was at the show the whole time.'

'Pity they've all scattered,' Toye remarked gloomily.

'Well, we know where the other lecturers are, anyway. It looks like a trip over to Crowncliff tomorrow. But I'm in no state to make plans until I've eaten, are you? Let's drop in at the station, and then track down some food.'

Later, having set in motion enquiries about Geoff Boothby at Birmingham University and Warhampton, on Superintendent Bostock's advice they made for the grill room of one of the Winnage hotels. After a satisfactory meal they settled in a corner of the lounge. Pollard threw himself into a chair, and for some time smoked in silence, his eyes closed.

Toye, who seldom relaxed unless officially off duty, eyed him at intervals.

'They'll ring us from the station if anything comes through from Pike about those three other chaps, I suppose?' he ventured at last.

'I'm not asleep,' Pollard remarked. 'In fact, what brain I've got has been ticking over steadily. You know, we aren't clear about the lie of the land at St Julitta's—literally, I mean. I suppose there's a school hall, and they'd have had the films in it. How easy would it have been for Boothby to slip in and out of it without being noticed? Was the schemozzle with the cars visible from inside the building? Is it really likely that with between eighty and ninety people milling around, no one ran into him as he went into the library, and finally came out again and went up to his room?'

'Depends on which bits of the places are used for what, doesn't it?'

'Yea. We'll apply to Mrs Makepeace. That suggests another run down to Kittitoe as the next thing on the list, and I've also had a thought about the Stubbs-Glover-Medlicott trio.'

Toye looked at him enquiringly.

'My Aunt Is. Before she retired she was a big noise in social welfare. She's had a good deal of experience of off-beat types. And she's got a link with all those three: Stubbs and Glover are fellow governors, and Medlicott is employed by the school. If I can get her to chat off the record, it might be very useful. Another pointer to Kittitoe tomorrow. But on the other hand, Boothby's the centre of the picture at the moment, and the most Boothby-conscious people at Kittitoe would be the bunch of Horner staff over at Crowncliff. They're more likely to have noticed him around—or not around—than anyone else.'

'Then there's that statement of Boothby's that he ran up against Jay's car when he was trying to get his own out,' Toye said thoughtfully. 'If he did, you'd expect something in the way of a scratch or a dent. We could have a look.'

'And it's possible Jay may have noticed that Austin 1100, and knows who it belongs to. It would save time. If Boothby did force its window, he probably damaged it. All told, it'd better be Crowncliff first.'

Pollard yawned and stretched.

'Do you swallow all that about Boothby falling flat for Wendy Shaw, more or less on sight?' Toye asked, after a pause. 'Shouldn't have thought she'd have bowled a chap over like that from her photo, and what we've heard about her.'

'Not most chaps, perhaps,' Pollard agreed, 'but Boothby isn't exactly run of the mill. Unconventional on the surface, but he's got definite values underneath. Remember what Mrs Makepeace said about him? She stressed how kind he'd been to these Fortnight people, the dim types particularly. I think pity for Wendy probably came into it in a big way…it mightn't have worked in the long run, you know…'

On their return to Stoneham a piece of the complicated jigsaw slipped satisfactorily into position. The forensic laboratory reported that the fragment of scarlet material salvaged in Beckon Cove was, beyond doubt, from Wendy Shaw's anorak.

9

Here a little, and there a little.

Isaiah. Chapter 28 verse 10

The Horner Hotel, Crowncliff, correctly conveyed the impression that the guiding principle behind its construction had been to cater for as many inmates as possible with the minimum of labour. It was an uncompromising cube of white stucco, chromium and glass, in a recently developed area on the outskirts of the town.

On arrival Pollard and Toye found immediate evidence of a Horner Discovery Fortnight in full swing. The available parking space was crowded with cars, most of which had recently experienced rough going. As Toye edged his way into a gap, a party emerged from the hotel armed with prawning nets, glass jars and note books. Its members were brick red from sunburn, and wore sunglasses and sexually indistinguishable clothing. Arguing animatedly among themselves, they set off in the direction of the shore. Another group stood silently round a car, contemplating a small object on its roof. As Pollard and Toye walked past, a man with a beard picked the object up reverently between finger and thumb.

'Indisputably an artefact,' he boomed.

Inside the hotel the foyer was lined with notice boards mounted on stands. Two of these supported a huge large-scale map of the locality. Others proffered information about lectures, discussion groups, expeditions, film shows, and local attractions ranging from church services of all denominations to pop concerts. There were hastily scribbled items under LOST and FOUND. Two notices in heavy black type urged Fortnighters to be on time for meals, and to park their cars with consideration for others. After a thoughtful survey Toye remarked that it wasn't his idea of a holiday.

There were distant sounds of a single voice raised didactically, and the clattering of crockery, but no sign of life or of any means of summoning attention.

'We'd better try a spot of discovery ourselves,' Pollard said, heading for a corridor.

As he spoke a door opened, and a man appeared who came quickly forward on sighting them.

'Sorry!' he exclaimed. 'Superintendent Pollard, isn't it? I hope you haven't been hanging around long. I'm Jay.'

'Good morning,' Pollard replied. 'No, we've only just arrived. It's an inconvenient visit, I'm afraid. There seems to be a good deal going on.'

'It hasn't been too difficult to switch things round so that you can meet the four of us who were at Kittitoe,' Michael Jay told him. 'Shall we go along to my office?'

The improvised office was businesslike, but with welcoming touches of fresh flowers and gay posters. As the three men sat round a table neatly stacked with files and folders, it occurred to Pollard that the room reflected its tenant. The Fortnight's Director was comfortably solid in build, with a pleasant face, but his competence and authority was also apparent.

Having declined refreshment, Pollard came straight to the point.

'Mrs Makepeace,' he opened, 'told me that it was on your advice that she made a statement to me about Mr Boothby.'

'That is correct,' Michael Jay answered. 'I want to say, though, that knowing Geoff Boothby as I do, I find any idea of him being involved in a murder sheer fantasy. My motive in advising Mrs Makepeace was to get his acquaintance with Wendy Shaw—for what it was worth—out into the open, rather than wait for you people to ferret it out.'

'A very sensible line to take, if I may say so, Mr Jay. I now have to tell you that we have already interviewed Mr

Boothby. He freely admits having met Wendy Shaw on a number of occasions during the Kittitoe Fortnight, and also that he drove up to Uncharted Seas after the film show at the school on the night of Friday, August 20.'

Michael Jay's head jerked up, but he said nothing.

'He went in the hopes of seeing Wendy Shaw,' Pollard went on, 'although she had told him when they were out together on the previous evening that she did not want a further meeting. He states that he was not admitted, and we have a witness who saw him coming away from the drive of Uncharted Seas at approximately ten-fifteen.'

He watched Michael Jay make a rapid calculation, and look relieved.

'All the same,' he continued, 'you'll appreciate the importance of our establishing the exact time at which he left St Julitta's. Did you by any chance see him drive off? I understand that his car, yours, and one other were parked immediately to the left of the front door as you go out.'

'Yes, they were, but I was nowhere near the front entrance at that time, damn it.' Michael Jay pushed aside a portable typewriter, and rested his elbows on the table, cupping his chin in his hands, and frowning as he talked. 'You see, the film show was in the school assembly hall, down at the west end of the building—that's the Beckon Head end, if you haven't got your orientation. I watched the films from the gallery, and as soon as they were over, went down to congratulate Paul King, who'd made them. Then I helped move people along to the common rooms for tea and coffee. We were running late, and I knew Mrs Makepeace was anxious about her women getting off. The common rooms are next to the hall, and I stayed in one or other of them with the crowd until nearly eleven.'

'I see,' Pollard said, concealing disappointment. 'Then we must count you out as far as the time Mr Boothby left goes. Did you notice him in the hall during the film show?'

'He wasn't in the gallery, but I was sitting in the back row, and couldn't see who was downstairs, except for people in the very front. He wasn't among those, as far as I remember.'

Leaving this topic Pollard turned to Geoff Boothby's return to the school. He learnt that at ten-thirty most of the

101

Fortnighters were still in the common rooms, in one of which community singing had started up. A few of the more elderly had departed, presumably to their rooms.

'Mr Boothby says that on coming in, he went into the library for about ten minutes, and then went up to bed. During this time he states that he met no one at all. Does this surprise you?'

'That's a difficult question to answer. As I said just now, most people were still in the common rooms. It doesn't seem likely that anyone was using the library, and all books taken out had been checked in on Thursday. I think I'd say there was a fifty-fifty chance of him running into somebody when he went upstairs, but the sick bay where his room was is a bit off the map.'

'Can we go back to the film show?' Pollard said. 'Did you notice anyone come in or go out while the show was on?'

'Mrs Makepeace came into the gallery about twenty minutes late, when she'd had her own dinner after ours,' Michael Jay replied with studied casualness. 'I'm sure nobody else came or went in the gallery, but I can't answer for downstairs. There was taped music going on, and a fair amount of applause and laughter at intervals.'

And I bet your attention was pretty fully occupied other than with the films, Pollard thought. He asked some questions about the later part of the evening, and heard that the common room parties had broken up by soon after eleven. After taking a look round, Michael Jay had gone to his office to deal with some paper work, and at ten minutes past twelve had locked the front door and gone up to his bedroom in the sick bay. There was no light under his neighbours' doors, so he had assumed that both of them had turned in. The custom was that anyone intending to be out after twelve left a note in his office, and he had found none. Asked about the extent of his final look round, he said that he went into the ground floor rooms used that evening, excluding the kitchen premises, which were Mrs Makepeace's province. No, she had not been in her office when he made his tour of inspection. It had a glass door, and he would have noticed a light there. Besides, she had said good night to him and gone up to bed earlier on.

'You may think this an odd request,' Pollard said, 'but may we take a look at your car?'

Michael Jay stared at him in astonishment.

'By all means,' he said. 'Come outside.'

As at St Julitta's, a parking space near the front door had been reserved for cars belonging to the staff. In it were a dark blue Hillman, a shabby estate car, and a scarlet mini. There was also a sizeable gap.

'This one's mine,' Michael Jay said, going up to the Hillman. 'Shall I run her out for you?'

'Please,' Pollard replied. 'Is this how the staff cars were parked at the school?'

'More or less. The mini belongs to the girl who's the equivalent of Geoff in this area. And the Kings' dormobile was parked round at the back, as they were sleeping in it. They prefer to, if any privacy's available.'

He reversed the Hillman clear of the adjacent cars, and got out. Pollard and Toye scrutinized the coachwork of the off side, finally concentrating on an area over the rear mudguard with a lens.

'This small scrape here is recent,' Pollard said, as they straightened up. 'Any idea when and where you got it?'

'Not within a day or two,' Michael Jay replied, looking baffled. 'I first spotted it last Monday, when I filled up with petrol for the run up here from Cornwall. I didn't have the car out last Sunday, and had driven down there from Kittitoe on the Saturday, as you know.'

'Was the car standing out while you were in Cornwall?'

'No. They gave me a lock-up.'

Pollard considered.

'Did you have the car out for the expedition on Friday?'

'No. I went over to Starbury in Geoff Boothby's car. The Kings and Miss Crump travelled with the coach parties. The last time I had mine out at Kittitoe was on the Friday morning. I ran into Winnage for various oddments, and took in petrol for Cornwall. I'm pretty sure I hadn't been biffed then. I can remember walking round the car at the petrol station, and taking a look at the tyres, and I'm fairly observant. I suppose one mustn't ask what all this is in aid of?'

'Tell you shortly,' Pollard replied. 'Just a few more points.

How exactly were the staff cars at the front of the school parked? I mean which way on, and in what order?'

Michael Jay screwed up his eyes in an attempt to visualize.

'All three nose to wall, always. Susan Crump next to the front door, Geoff next to the library, and mine in the middle, as I'm the most careful driver, and it was a tight fit.'

Pollard rested his arms on the roof of the Hillman, and looked across it at its owner.

'What I'm leading up to is this,' he said. 'Mr Boothby states that after coming out of the front door at the end of the film show, he had difficulty in backing out his car. Somebody had parked an Austin 1100 outside the library bay, slightly overlapping him. He had a couple of shots, in the second of which he says he just touched your car. He then abandoned the attempt, and finally managed to force one of the Austin's windows which was open a little, and get the brake off.'

Michael Jay stared at him.

'But surely this is frightfully important,' he exclaimed. 'I mean, if he was seen coming away from Horner's place at a quarter past ten, and was held up over getting away from the school, surely he's in the clear on the time score? I can swear that the films weren't over until ten to ten.'

'I'm afraid it's not conclusive. It could be argued that he noticed the scrape when loading up his own car to leave on Saturday morning, and saw how he could turn it to account. Then there's also the possibility of his having paid an earlier visit to the bungalow, during the film show. So far no one has witnessed to his being present. Going back to the forcing of the Austin's window, we think that forcing it would have left traces of damage, and want to contact its owner. Can you remember who owned a car of that type on the Kittitoe Fortnight?'

Michael Jay groaned, and clutched at his thick black hair.

'Hell, I just can't! Not offhand, anyway. When you're constantly coping with fresh batches of people, the last lot just falls out of your mind. Perhaps one of the others might remember...here come the Kings, anyway.'

A green dormobile had turned into the drive, and was

being edged into its allotted space. Pollard gazed at it, momentarily distracted by thoughts of family holidays when the twins were a year or two older...it would be a real moneysaver...

He pulled himself together as a man and a woman scrambled out, wearing jeans and windcheaters, and with cameras and binoculars slung round their necks. They looked anxiously towards Michael Jay and himself, and were introduced as Paul and Janice King.

'Hope we haven't held things up,' the man said. 'We've left the pack down on the estuary, Mike, and told 'em to make their own way back.'

'Help me shove the bus back,' Michael Jay said, 'and we'll go along to the office.'

Pollard took stock. Paul King, with pale sandy hair and rather sharp features, had vitality and intelligence, he thought, but looked temperamental. Janice King he put down as a hardboiled but competent little piece. Back in the office he sensed a change of atmosphere. It was as though the three Horner staff had drawn together, and his official status was more in evidence. Involuntarily he became more formal.

'For the benefit of Mr and Mrs King,' he said, 'I will restate the purpose of our visit here. Certain facts about Wendy Shaw's murder are now definitely known to us. She was alive and acting perfectly normally at eight o'clock. At about a quarter past ten there was no answer to a telephone call to the bungalow. At eleven-forty, when Mr Horner, his daughter and son-in-law returned, she was nowhere to be found. From these facts it seems reasonable to deduce that by about ten-fifteen she was either already murdered, or had left the bungalow with her killer. We also know,' he went on, conscious of the three pairs of eyes fixed upon him, 'that various people were in the vicinity of Uncharted Seas after eight o'clock on that evening. One of these, Mr Geoffrey Boothby, admits that he drove there after your film show at St Julitta's.'

'Geoff!' Paul King exclaimed incredulously.

'He would land himself up to the neck in something like this,' Janice King commented, with a slight edge of contempt on her voice. 'Poor old Geoff! Too utterly fantastic!'

'We know when Mr Boothby left the bungalow,' Pollard resumed. 'What we are trying to establish is at what time he arrived there. Mr Jay did not see him leave the school premises. Did either of you?'

He looked enquiringly from husband to wife. Paul King, scowling deeply, slowly rubbed his forehead with the back of his hand.

'No,' he said. 'I can't remember seeing a sign of him after dinner. To begin with I was editing film in the lab I was using as a dark room, and didn't emerge with the finished product until about twenty to nine. I didn't notice him in the audience, or going out of the show at the end. I went along to a sort of farewell do in the common rooms afterwards, and they're nowhere near the front entrance.'

'What about you, Mrs King?' Pollard asked.

She gave a faintly provocative shrug.

'Honestly, I don't think I'd have noticed my own Mum around that evening,' she told him. 'We were late back from the expedition, and people had got a bit wet, and the fuss-pots were certain they'd develop pneumonia. Then I had to cope with the projector and what-have-you, as Paul was still editing the blasted Fortnight film. You see, he—'

'Perhaps Mr King would tell us about this himself,' Pollard interrupted her, politely but firmly.

'Entirely my own fault,' Paul King said irritably. 'I ought to have done the processing of the last film on the Thursday night, and the bulk of the editing on Friday morning, before we started for Starbury Bay. As it was, I was asked to join a party at the pub after dinner, and left the processing till Friday morning, banking on having ample time to edit the thing, and integrate it with the film as a whole after we got back from Starbury. The result was that I couldn't get the job done by dinner time, and we had to put on a short film to keep people amused until I was ready.'

'I see,' said Pollard. 'Do I take it, then, that neither of you noticed Mr Boothby during the show itself, or going off afterwards, or, for that matter, coming in later?'

Both the Kings shook their heads.

'He certainly wasn't in the common rooms,' Janice said.

106

'Of course, he isn't the matey type, and apt to slope off on purely social occasions, isn't he, Mike?'

Michael Jay, looking worried and unhappy, agreed.

'First-rate on the work side of a Fortnight, but not much help over the get-togethers,' he added rather absently.

From further questioning Pollard established that the Kings had gone off to bed themselves when the parties first showed signs of breaking up, at about a quarter to eleven, and had not needed to pass through the entrance hall to go out to their dormobile.

'My God, this is simply awful,' Michael Jay burst out suddenly. 'Obviously the idea of Geoff having killed anybody is simply ludicrous, yet none of us can produce the simple bits of information that would remove him from the picture altogether. Somebody simply must have seen him around. Damn it, there were about ninety people milling about.'

'If it proves necessary,' Pollard said calmly, 'we shall question every one of them. By the way, were any outsiders invited to the festivities on the last evening?'

'I managed to ring Andrew Medlicott when we decided to put on the short bird film,' Janice said. 'He came along, but I don't know of anyone else, do you?'

She looked at Michael Jay and her husband, both of whom replied in the negative.

'Did Mr Medlicott stay on for refreshments in the common rooms?' Pollard asked.

'Oh, no. He's a poppet, but as shy as they come. Paul and I only got to know him because he's taken up bird watching.'

The sound of tramping feet and loud conversation came from the corridor.

'That's Susan's lecture finishing,' Michael Jay said, getting up and going to the door. 'Here she comes.'

As he spoke, a stocky figure in slacks and a crumpled cotton top appeared on the threshold.

'These the sleuths?' she demanded, indicating Pollard and Toye.

'Come in, and meet Superintendent Pollard and Inspector Toye of Scotland Yard,' Michael Jay said. 'Miss Susan Crump, gentlemen. And I hope to God she'll be a bit more help than the rest of us have been,' he added heavily.

Susan Crump stared at him.

'For heaven's sake, Mike! What goes on?'

'At the moment, Miss Crump,' Pollard told her, 'we're anxious to find out if Mr Boothby was present at the film show on the last Friday of the Kittitoe Fortnight, and at what time he drove away from the school to go and see Wendy Shaw at Uncharted Seas, as he admits to have done.'

'Geoff?' she exclaimed, thrusting a straggling lock of greying hair out of her eyes. 'Bonkers! If you're hounding Geoff Boothby, you're wasting your time, let me tell you, not to mention the taxpayers' money. I haven't the remotest idea when he went out—I was down at the assembly hall end of the place after the show. But he was in the show all right, the whole time. He was sitting with that schoolmaster chap from Essex who brought two of his boys to the Fortnight. Yates, wasn't he called? They were a couple of rows in front of me.'

There was a brief tense silence, broken by her three colleagues all speaking at once.

When Susan Crump and the Kings had gone, Michael Jay looked across the table at Pollard.

'I've remembered the name of that couple who owned the Austin 1100,' he said. 'Gedge, they were called. And I'm almost sure they were Londoners. Head Office will have their address, of course.'

'You're discreet, Mr Jay,' Pollard remarked approvingly. 'Most people would have shouted it out the moment it came into their heads.'

'I kept my mouth shut on principle, may I say? There was no particular significance about it.'

'I take your point,' Pollard told him. 'Got that list of cars and their owners that Mrs Makepeace gave us, Toye?'

Toye had already extracted it from the file, and passed it over.

'Here we are,' Pollard said, running his eye down the typewritten sheet. 'Streatham...telephone number and all. Good for the Horner organization. We're grateful, Mr Jay. This is going to save valuable time. And now we'll remove ourselves,

108

and ring these people from the local station.'

As he escorted them to their car, Michael Jay expressed the hope that Mrs Makepeace would be able to get away from Kittitoe as soon as possible.

'Quite apart from all the work she did for the Fortnight, this business has been pretty grim for her,' he said, 'especially having been the means of the body being found.'

Pollard assured him that Mrs Makepeace had already been told that as far as the police were concerned, there was nothing to detain her at the school.

'The romance you're sponsoring seems to be going ahead all right,' he remarked to Toye, as they drove off.

'They'd match up nicely, I'd say,' Toye allowed.

At the Crowncliff police station they ran into the familiar hold-up of getting no reply to their telephone call, and a second attempt after a hasty lunch was also unsuccessful. Pollard then rang the Yard, asking for the Gedges to be located at the earliest possible moment, adding that he was just about to start back to Stoneham, and could be contacted there.

On the way they discussed the information gathered at Crowncliff. On the credit side it could now be accepted that Geoff Boothby had not paid an earlier visit to the bungalow during the film show. If the delay he claimed to have had in setting off for Uncharted Seas afterwards could also be established, he could be crossed off the list of suspects. In this connection both men agreed that, in itself, the damage to Michael Jay's car was inconclusive as evidence, but it would reinforce the significance of a damaged window in the Gedges' Austin.

The unexpected presence of Andrew Medlicott at the entertainment was rather interesting.

'Where do you suppose the chap was between 9.50 pm, and the time that couple driving home from Biddle Bay saw him coming out of one or t'other of the drive gates?' Toye asked.

'God knows,' Pollard replied.

He relapsed into a lengthy silence, his thoughts revolving round the rather enigmatic figure of the bursar. It occurred to him again that inadequate knowledge of the school building was being a handicap, making it difficult to visualize the numerous comings and goings on the night of the murder. Another visit to St Julitta's was indicated...

Depression began to envelop him. Suppose Boothby were cleared, and Andrew Medlicott able to prove that he'd put in an hour and a half over accounts in his office? One would be left with Hugh Stubbs and his obsessions, and that bull at a gate, Glover...It was human personality that made investigation so hellishly complicated...people's fears, so often irrational, and the infinite variety of outlets found by their innate aggressiveness...even more, the fact that the great majority were genuinely unconscious of what made them tick...

'The real murderer of Wendy Shaw is that pathetic bloody mother of hers,' he suddenly said aloud.

Toye looked startled. Then, in his careful conscientious way, he mulled over this proposition.

'I get you, sir,' he said, after so long an interval that Pollard's mind had moved on to another topic.

On arriving at Stoneham in mid-afternoon, they learnt that prompt action by the Yard had produced only a negative result. The Gedges' house in Streatham was shut up, and the neighbour in charge of the key reported that they were touring Cornwall, and not expected back until the weekend. She did not know on which day.

'Too vague,' Pollard said. 'We'll get a police message on the air this evening.'

While this was being dealt with, he came to a decision.

'Look here,' he said to Toye, 'I want you to hang on here tonight. The Gedges or some local station may ring in. If so, get the Gedges along here with their car, or along to me if more convenient for them. I'll go on down, and put up with my aunt—here's her phone number. She's a local, and a governor of the school, and I want to see what I can pick up about the Stubbs-Glover-Medlicott bunch, to get some sort of a starting point on each of them. I know we've had a certain amount from Pike, but I feel I'd like a bit more. There's not much my revered aunt misses. Ring me first thing tomorrow about our next move. OK?'

Toye, who enjoyed a little scope for independent action, concurred.

'Right, then,' Pollard said. 'I'll ring her straight away.'

He got through without difficulty.

'Tom here, Aunt Is,' he told her. 'Speaking from Stoneham, and taking you up on your offer. Can I have a bed tonight?... No, only me. Inspector Toye's staying up here. I'll eat on the way down, of course.'

'You'll do nothing of the sort,' Miss Isabel Dennis's voice came crisply over the line. 'There'll be a proper meal waiting for you here.'

'Short notice, isn't it?'

'Aha! I've changed the car for a mini.'

'Changed the car for a mini?' he echoed.

'To make room in the garage for a deep freeze, my lad.'

10

Why faintest thou?
>   Matthew Arnold. *Thyrsis.*

Suddenly a long melancholy bellow rose and fell, hanging in the air as if reluctant to die away.

'Sorry you've come in for this,' Isabel Dennis remarked. 'One soon gets used to it, though. There's been a fog bank out at sea all day. It's moving in now—look.'

Pollard turned in his chair to see strands of white mist hurrying soundlessly past the window.

'Glad I got down here when I did,' he said.

'Black or white?' enquired his aunt from behind the coffee percolator.

'Black, please. May I smoke?'

'If it's essential to your well-being. I'm glad to see you've cut down.'

He grinned at her, lit up, and reclined contentedly with his long legs stretched out to a small log fire, feeling well fed and relaxed. Cosy but uncluttered, he thought, looking round the room with its crimson carpet and its white walls. The haphazard alcoves you got in these old cottages were perfect for pieces of good china...Trust Aunt Is to make a smooth job of her retirement home. Night storage heaters, a deep freeze...the lot. He transferred his gaze to Isabel Dennis herself, and decided that intelligence and character in a woman's face wore better than conventional good looks. Jane would want to paint her, sitting so upright in that straightbacked chair, with her crisp grey hair and lively dark eyes.

'How tiresome that the powers that be had to pick on you for this case,' she remarked.

'Why, aunt? Is having your policeman nephew around making you feel conspicuous?'

'Not in the least. At least, it is, and I'm enjoying it. No, it's only that I'm afraid you mayn't want to bring Jane and the children down next summer after being here professionally.'

'Actually, I haven't been involved with many of the locals,' he said. 'It's been the Horner crowd mostly. Is this let to Horner an annual affair?'

'Oh, no. It's the first time ever, only arising because his hotel at Biddle Bay was damaged by fire. Normally we let for one fortnight only, to a children's home from the Midlands.'

'He's paying you through the nose for the place, I suppose?' Pollard looked at her quizzically.

'Of course he is. All the same, I wish we could put the clock back. It's turned out more hindrance than let, and the antis on the governing body are crowing like cocks.'

'On what grounds were they anti? I should have thought it was a very sound scheme.'

Isabel Dennis's quick glance flicked over him.

'The Old Girls' representative thought it might be infra dig for St Julitta's to get involved with a popular set-up like Horner's Holidays. Hugh Stubbs, the founder of the Kittitoe Residents' Association, was convinced that it would bring in a swarm of undesirables, and lower the tone of the village. He's being insufferable at the moment.'

'Tell me some more about this apprehensive chap,' Pollard invited.

'He's a retired civil servant, who settled here some years back, picking up a derelict village house, and modernising it to Ideal Home standard. He feels threatened, and his defensive action has turned him into a local menace.'

'How threatened?'

Isabel Dennis was silent for a moment, and turning her head slightly, met her nephew's gaze.

'This is only my purely personal opinion, Tom,' she said emphatically.

113

'Fair enough, Aunt Is,' he replied reassuringly. 'Let's have it, all the same.'

'As I see it, he feels his whole way of life is being undermined by the general upheaval that's going on—technological, political, social, moral—you know. Hence the Kittitoe Residents' Association, which works to prevent as far as possible any change in the place, and to keep the holiday industry as select as possible. More coffee?'

'Thanks, I will. It's super.' Pollard handed her his cup, and waited for it to be filled. 'But there's something to be said for a KRA, surely?' he went on. 'I mean, it's a lovely little village, and development ought to be carefully planned. That frightful caravan site's gone quite far enough in the wrong direction.'

'Of course, there's a great deal to be said for a KRA of the right sort. But if you overdo the conservation idea, it so easily interferes with people's liberty, and anyway defeats its own ends by putting their backs up. That's what Hugh Stubbs is doing. He's become quite unbalanced about the village, and his wife's almost as bad. He's heading for trouble,' Isabel Dennis concluded vigorously.

'What sort of trouble? Somebody taking him to court?'

'More likely somebody beating him up. One aspect of all this is that on the pretext of maintaining decent standards of behaviour in the place during the summer holiday season, he's apparently becoming a Peeping Tom.'

Pollard looked up sharply at this echo of Constable Pike and Toye.

'Is there any real evidence of this?' he asked.

'Yes, I think one can say there is. It's been quite openly talked about lately, even up here, in Holston. My woman's son took his current girl friend down to the Biddle Bay sand dunes one evening recently, and according to her, Hugh Stubbs came creeping up on them. And I happened to see something decidedly odd happening last week. On the night of that poor child's murder, as a matter of fact.'

'Which was?'—Pollard prompted.

'Well, I think you know I've taken up bellringing as a retirement hobby. We haven't a peal here, so I ring down at Kittitoe. Our weekly practice is normally on Thursdays, from

8.30 to 9.30 in the evening. Last week it was changed to Friday because of a cricket match. I dropped in at the Vicarage afterwards, and came away soon after ten. As I drove out on to the Biddle Bay road, my headlights picked up a stationary car on the edge of the dunes. I was coming up to it when a man appeared running towards it, chased by another who was picking up stones and flinging them at him. As I drew up, I saw Hugh Stubbs scramble into the car, and the other man saw me and turned tail. There was a dog barking inside. It was the stickiest moment. I accelerated, and only trust Hugh Stubbs was too het up to recognize me. I watched in the driving mirror as I went on, and saw him drive off towards the village.'

'I'm not going to pretend that this isn't important,' Pollard said after a brief pause. 'Can you possibly be a bit more exact about times?'

Isabel Dennis leant forward and put another log on the fire with deliberate care.

'Now I think back, I remember hearing the church clock strike ten when I was in the vicarage,' she said. 'It's usually about two minutes fast. It was very soon afterwards that I got up to go. Arthur Fuller came with me to the door, and we stood nattering, but not for long. I must have left at six or seven minutes past ten, and it's no distance to where Hugh Stubbs had parked. Say I saw it all happening at ten minutes past.'

'Did you see any other cars as you came away? Parked, or on the road?'

'No, I'm sure of that. It was raining, and the road was deserted.'

Pollard stubbed out his cigarette, and lit another.

'About the chap who was chasing Stubbs,' he said, 'did you recognize him?'

'No. He moved like a young man. I concluded at the time that Hugh Stubbs had been snooping, and found him with a girl in the shelter.'

'Shelter?'

'Yes. One of those seaside things with a lot of glass, and seats for people to enjoy the view. There's one quite close to where the car was parked.'

'That makes the snooping theory more convincing, doesn't it, in view of the weather? I mean fun and games in the sand hills would hardly have been on.'

Pollard spoke abstractedly, his mind on the timetable drawn up with Toye. This timing was just right for the near miss with Boothby's car, and the arrival of both parties at the King William, vouched for by Nancekivell...Was it even imaginable that if Stubbs had already been up to Uncharted Seas and murdered Wendy Shaw, that he'd go on to do a bit of snooping?

He switched to another topic.

'Aunt Is,' he said suddenly, 'are you absolutely certain, beyond any doubt, that the chap chasing Stubbs wasn't Don Glover?'

Their eyes met squarely.

'Absolutely, and beyond any doubt, Tom,' she replied firmly. 'I deduce that you've been told that they're at each other's throats?'

'I have. I've also met Mr Glover. Separated him and Constable Pike, in fact. How about the lowdown on him?'

'You know, I rather like Don Glover,' Isabel Dennis said. 'He's terribly brash, and often behaves outrageously, but he's got good points. Vitality, for instance, and he can be very generous.'

'Pretty warm, I gather?'

'Oh, yes. A very capable and prosperous business man, with his finger in any number of local pies. But in other ways he's more like a child. Desperately anxious to cut a figure, you know. The trouble is that he isn't persona grata with the social circle he thinks he ought to be in—he just hasn't got what it takes, and can't see it. Hence the aggressiveness and the pushing.'

'I can see that the siting of that caravan colony of his isn't likely to have made him popular.'

'It certainly hasn't, and there's a frightful rumour going round that he's trying to buy the land further up the hill, in order to expand the place.'

'Good God! Let's hope the Planning people put paid to that one. There seem to be so many loopholes, though, and I bet he's got a smart lawyer. Going back to his social life, he's apparently on visiting terms with Mr Horner.'

'I'm surprised to hear that. Now I come to think of it, though, Don Glover backed the let so hard at a governors' meeting that it nearly ended in us all voting against it.'

'Do you think,' Pollard asked, suddenly struck by an idea, 'that they've got business interests in common?'

'Unlikely, I should say. Don Glover's interests are all local, and pretty small beer by the side of Horner's Holidays.'

Pollard put his idea on one side for later consideration, and moved on rather cautiously to the subject of Andrew Medlicott. After all, Aunt Is was one of the chap's employers...

'Running a place like St Julitta's must involve quite a bit of administration,' he said casually. 'Who copes with the finances?'

'A small sub-committee of the governing body. We have a bursar for the routine work.'

'Medlicott, he's called, isn't he? I ran into him the other day.'

'Yes. He's one of these unfortunate redundant executives in their fifties. We were very lucky to get him. He's extremely competent. The only snag is that he's an appalling worrier, and always takes the gloomiest view. This business has shattered him: he's convinced that all the parents will remove their children because of the school's name being brought in.'

'Afraid of another job folding, I expect.' Pollard stifled a yawn.

His aunt eyed him.

'Why not put through a call to Jane while I get you a nightcap? You look as though you could do with a good night's sleep.'

The first part of this programme was enjoyably carried through, but once in bed, Pollard lay awake for some time milling over his recent idea about Don Glover. Was the chap's unconvincing story about an abortive business trip to Biddle Bay really covering up an abortive one to Uncharted Seas? Had he kept quiet about the latter for fear of being caught up in the investigation of the murder? An unpremeditated trip at 10.30 pm would suggest that he was on quite intimate terms with Eddy Horner—it must have been un-premeditated, because otherwise he would have known that Eddy was going to Stoneham, and wouldn't he have known, if they knew each other well? Pollard wondered if the Stoneham trip was a regular Friday night fixture while Penny Townsend and the baby were at Kittitoe, and her husband working at the Horner office in London during the week? If so, quite a lot of people might have known that Wendy would be alone with the baby for some hours on the evening of her murder...

Of course, motive's been the baffling thing all along, he thought, if one rules out a homicidal maniac of one sort or another. Attempted robbery interrupted by Wendy makes much more sense, but then there's the complete absence of any trace of it, especially with that damned woman cleaning the place the next morning...

At the thought of the almost limitless field of suspects opened up by the attempted robbery idea he groaned aloud, and heaved himself on to his other side, cursing the reiter-ated booming of the foghorn. Utterly preposterous in the radar age...

Presently the recurring sound assumed a rhythm, and he slid into sleep.

Apparently without passage of time there was a brisk rattle of curtains being drawn back, and a flood of bright light in the room.

'The fog's cleared,' Isabel Dennis announced. 'Here's a cuppa for you. I hope you've had a good sleep. I'm just about to have breakfast with Inspector Toye and a nice young constable who's run him down from Stoneham. You needn't hurry—your bacon and eggs are in the simmering oven.'

'Good lord!' Pollard exclaimed, sitting up hastily, and trying to adjust himself. 'I must have slept like the dead.'

'Excellent for the little grey cells,' said his aunt, as she withdrew.

Pollard speculated on what had brought Toye down post haste, while he shaved, bathed and dressed. He was almost ready when he heard sounds of departure, and a car starting up in the street outside, presumably the nice young constable going off. Running downstairs to the kitchen, he found Toye at the toast and marmalade stage, and his aunt stacking crockery in the dishwasher.

'Here you are,' she said, producing a heaped plate, and pouring out coffee. 'I'll leave you both to get on with it while I start my chores.'

'Very good indeed of Miss Dennis to lay on a slap-up breakfast like this,' Toye remarked, as he returned from politely closing the door behind his hostess. 'I appreciate it, and so did the young chap.'

'Bet it's your second breakfast of the day,' Pollard said, taking up his knife and fork. 'What's the big idea behind this turning up at daybreak?'

'The Gedges, sir. A patrol spotted them on the road at two o'clock this morning, about a dozen miles out of Stoneham, and brought them along to the station. That car window's jammed all right. I tested it myself.'

It appeared that the Gedges had decided to return home a day early, and to drive through the night, avoiding the crowded roads of a Bank Holiday weekend. They had no car radio, and had not heard any broadcasts on the previous evening. Toye, roused from his bed by a telephone call to the hotel, had found them excited, and tiresomely facetious, but perfectly coherent when questioned. The gist of their statement was that when they left Kittitoe on the morning of Saturday, August 21, they had found the passenger window of their car jammed, leaving a gap of about three inches at the top. As it was raining hard, they had stopped at the first sizeable garage for repairs, only to be told that it was quite a big job, and couldn't possibly be dealt with on the busiest Saturday morning of the year. There had been nothing for it but pushing on, with the gap stuffed up to the best of their ability. The weather had improved on Sunday and not wanting to be without the car for the rest of their holiday, they had decided to risk it, and wait to have the window mended when they got home.

'Did they remember leaving the window open the night before?' Pollard asked.

'They had no end of argy-bargy about it at first,' Toye said disapprovingly. 'At the tops of their voices, too, in the middle of the night. In the end I got it clear that the last time they'd used the car on the Friday was before dinner. They'd run another couple down to the pub in Kittitoe for a quick one. It was when they were telling me this that Mrs Gedge gave a screech, and said she'd opened the window a bit on the way back to the school. The other three were smoking, and she wanted a breath of air. I said wouldn't she have shut it before leaving the car, as it was raining, and they laughed like drains, and said it was just like them to forget all about it, and have the car awash the next morning. Mr Gedge said they were nearly late for dinner, and had to dash for it.'

'Hence the careless parking, blocking Boothby, I suppose. Did you ask them if there were any signs of the car having been tampered with or moved, when they went out to it the next morning?'

'I asked 'em, all right, but short of a wheel missing, or the car being shifted to the far end of the drive, I don't think they'd have noticed a thing. Hit or miss types, they were. The coachwork was scraped and dented in half a dozen places, and you should have seen the muck inside. They just went on about what a yell it was baling out before they could start.'

'I suppose there's something to be said for that sort of outlook on life,' Pollard commented, taking another piece of toast. 'It's apt to pall on a third party at two am, though. But you've brought along a useful confirmation of Boothby's statement.'

'Do you reckon this lets him out, sir?' Toye asked.

'In my own mind, yes. But if possible, we've got to find somebody who saw the car shifting business. I've covered a bit of ground myself, by the way.'

He proceeded to pass on his aunt's account of the incident on the road to Biddle Bay, together with her comments on Hugh Stubbs, Don Glover and Andrew Medlicott.

'Looks as though Stubbs is going the way of Boothby,' Toye remarked. 'One lead after another petering out. If Stubbs really didn't leave home until a quarter to ten, and went straight back there when he left the pub car park, he's right out.'

'Right out,' Pollard agreed. 'Before we go along to the school this morning, we'll contact Pike. He may have picked up something about one or other of these chaps.'

Getting up from the breakfast table, he went in search of his aunt.

Constable Pike had managed to unearth one useful piece of information. A Kittitoe resident who lived in a cottage beyond Stubbs's house, and had walked past the latter just about half-past ten on the night of August 20, had seen his neighbour locking his garage after putting his car away. No, they hadn't spoken, having had words about putting out dustbins, but Pike's informant would swear to what he'd seen.

'Jolly good work, Pike,' Pollard said encouragingly. 'Now we know when he got home, I want you to drop all these other people for the moment, and try to find out where Mr Stubbs was between eight and ten that night. Let's have a look at your notes on his interview, Inspector.'

'Do Mr and Mrs Stubbs get their own supper?' Pollard said presently.

'That's right, sir,' Pike replied. 'They only have a woman in mornings.'

'What about the trivial telly programme he couldn't stomach?' asked Toye.

'If he was trying to cover his tracks, he could easily have got it from the Radio Times. Still, we might as well have a look. Have you still got last week's issue, Pike?'

After a search in the living room of the police house it was found, still intact. On August 20 the nine o'clock news had been followed by a sports programme.

'I suppose Mr Stubbs has a mind above the purely recreational,' Pollard said. 'Well, just go on slogging away, Pike. Inspector Toye and I are going along to the school.'

As they drove up to the front door of St Julitta's, a Morris 1000 was standing outside it with the boot open. The next moment Marcia Makepeace came out, and halted on seeing them.

'Good morning,' Pollard said, as he emerged and went towards her. 'I hope this means you're getting away at last?

We needn't hold you up at all. We just want to have a look at the rooms the Horner people used during the Fortnight. I'm sure the caretaker could show us.'

As he talked, it struck him that she looked younger, more confident—even gay. All this is slipping off her, he thought. I do believe she and Jay have definitely fixed it up...

Marcia was assuring him that she was in no hurry.

'I'm not making for London until Sunday,' she said, 'and the people I'm staying with aren't expecting me till lunchtime. Do come in, and I'll take you on an escorted tour.'

She was as good as her word. Pollard quickly realized that basically St Julitta's consisted of a central entrance hall with long wings running east and west. The main staircase led up from the hall to two upper floors, used for dormitories and staff accommodation on either side of central corridors. Each wing had a two-storey extension on its north side. That off the west wing had the kitchens on the ground floor, and the sick bay conveniently above, with a linking staircase. Pollard reflected that Geoff Boothby could have gone up to bed by that route, and might very well not have met anyone else. It was less public than the main staircase.

When they returned to the ground floor, a tour of the west wing cleared his mind at once about the movements of people after the film show on the evening of the murder. Almost everyone would have been concentrated there, the Fortnighters, Michael Jay, the Kings and Susan Crump in the common rooms, and the domestic staff still on duty in the kitchens and dealing with refreshments. There was no reason for anyone to be in the entrance hall, except the group going down to the pub, and a little behind them, Geoff Boothby. And, presumably, Andrew Medlicott, going home after contracting out from the common room party after the films.

Pollard suddenly stopped in his tracks. Had Andrew Medlicott gone home? If so, he had come out again, either to the school or to Uncharted Seas...

'Is there anything you'd like to have another look at?' Marcia Makepeace asked, who, like Toye, had also stopped.

'No, thanks,' Pollard replied, 'I was just recapping.'

'It's quite a pleasant entrance hall, isn't it?' she said, as they came into it again. 'I always wish they hadn't enclosed that bit of it, though.' She drew his attention to the area on the east of the front door, which had been walled off, and provided with a door with upper panels of glass leading into the east corridor. 'It makes the rest look a bit lopsided.'

'Why did they do it?' Pollard asked.

'Because of the need for more small rooms. Hotel ground floor rooms are so big as a rule. It's the bursar's office now. There used to be a bar there, I believe.'

With the conviction of being on the brink of something of major importance, Pollard followed her to the next door, and into the library. He gave a quick glance round, and exchanged another with Toye. After admiring the well-stocked shelves and ample table space, he strolled over to the window, and looked down on the space where the three staff cars had been parked.

The members of the Discovery Fortnight had used the library, but no other part of the east wing, beyond one classroom which had been Michael Jay's office, and a small laboratory used by Paul King for film processing and editing. The two wings were identical, the projection on the north side of the east wing housing laboratories and a studio on the ground floor, and bathrooms above, with a similar linking staircase.

Marcia Makepeace opened a door on to the level concreted area at the rear of the building, and pointed out the games field to the east. On the far side of the concrete the headland rose precipitously to the level of Uncharted Seas. Pollard glanced upwards. At this time, only a week ago, he thought, I'd never heard of the damned place...

'Thank you so much for taking us round, Mrs Makepeace,' he said, as they retraced their steps along the corridor to the front door. 'I suppose,' he went on, 'we couldn't possibly stay in the library for a spell, and get down to some paperwork? It's pretty cramped quarters in Constable Pike's place.'

'Why, of course,' she said. 'I'll just tell the caretakers that you're here. When you go, just slam the front door. We keep it on the catch during the day. Would you like some elevenses?'

'No thanks very much,' he said. 'We've had huge breakfasts at my aunt's. I expect you know her—Miss Isabel Dennis.'

'Indeed I do,' Marcia replied warmly. 'She's a splendid person. I'll never forget how kind she was to me when I first came.'

Ten minutes later she drove off, with a final wave of her hand to Pollard and Toye on the steps. They turned, and went into the hall.

'The key's on the outside of the door,' Pollard said, as they reached the bursar's office.

The next moment they were inside. It was meticulously orderly, with the unopened morning's post on the blotting pad of the kneehole desk.

'This is the hatch they shoved the drinks through to the people in the room that's now the library, I take it?' Toye asked.

Pollard pushed gently. A crack opened, giving a view of the window seat in the library.

'Quite right,' he said. 'And it was from here, I think, that Medlicott, for some unknown reason, snooped on Boothby. Instead of going home after the films he seems to have lurked in here. And with any luck, he saw Boothby shifting the cars. My God, here he comes—we'll have to play it by ear.'

The front door closed, and a quick, rather light step crossed the hall. There was a moment's delay as the new arrival tried to turn the key of the unlocked door of the office. Then he opened the door, and stood on the threshold, a man of medium height, greying, and with anxiety lines about his eyes. He crumpled soundlessly into a surprisingly small heap on the floor.

11

Presented with a universal blank.
Paradise Lost. Book Three

'Try a nip,' Pollard suggested, proffering brandy in the library. 'I stand to be reduced to the ranks for startling a respectable citizen like this,' he went on in a cheerful conversational tone, watching the colour creep back into Andrew Medlicott's face. 'Mrs Makepeace offered us houseroom in here for an hour or two, and it suddenly struck us that your office window overlooks something we're interested in—where some of the Horner staff parked their cars.'

'Sorry I was such a damn fool,' Andrew Medlicott muttered self-consciously. 'I-er-haven't been too fit lately.'

'Bad luck. Could you bear it if we did a bit of thinking aloud? It's just remotely possible that you could help us.'

'I'm perfectly all right now, thanks.'

'I expect you saw something of the Horner staff during the Fortnight?' Pollard asked. 'Did you register young Boothby?'

'Oh, yes. I met him socially up at Mr Horner's at the beginning, and saw him around the place once or twice afterwards.'

'He's made a statement which we haven't been able to get fully confirmed up to now. Part of it is that he left here after the film show on the night of Wendy Shaw's murder, but was held up a bit because he couldn't get his car out. Another car had been badly parked outside this window, and it was blocking him. Inspector Toye and I were over at

125

Crowncliff yesterday, where they're running another Discovery Fortnight, and somebody—Mrs King, I think—happened to mention that you were at the final film show. We were wondering just now if by any chance you went to your office afterwards, and happened to see Boothby shunting about?'

He met Andrew Medlicott's worried eyes, and smiled encouragingly.

'I did go into my office, as a matter of fact. Mrs King had asked me to join a gathering in the common rooms, but I'm not a sociable type, I'm afraid, and managed to get out of it...Yes, Boothby's car was making such a row that I looked out of the window. He tried backing, but couldn't make it. Then he got out, and went to the car that was blocking him. I couldn't see what he was doing, but he must have managed to get the brake off, and shift it. I suppose the owner hadn't locked it. It's staggering how careless people are.'

'Absolutely staggering,' Pollard agreed. 'It makes endless work for the police. How long would you say Boothby was held up over all this?'

'I'd find it very difficult to say exactly.' Andrew Medlicott became tense at being pinned down. 'You see, I've no idea how long he'd been trying to get clear before I noticed him. But I do remember looking at my watch after he'd managed it and driven off, and it was just turned ten o'clock.'

There was a momentary pause.

'You've helped us more than you can know at the moment,' Pollard said. 'Are we allowed to smoke in here, by the way?' he added, taking out his cigarette case.

'The Governors do...I keep some ash-trays in my office. Shall I—'

'Inspector Toye can put his hand on them, I expect.'

Under cover of small talk he cast around for his next opening until Toye returned.

'I suppose it's too much to hope that you stayed on in your office for a bit?' he hazarded.

'I did, actually,' Andrew Medlicott replied with notice-able unwillingness.

'Obviously you're observant. Could you cast your mind back and tell us anything, however trivial it seems, that you noticed going on inside or outside while you were still there? There's no hurry—take your time.'

To his surprise Andrew Medlicott seemed to find it easier to embark on a continuous statement than to answer a series of questions. It appeared that a good deal of noise was coming from the direction of the common rooms. After a bit people had come away from the west wing, and gone upstairs. Just before half-past ten Mrs Makepeace and Mr Jay had come along, and stood talking at the foot of the stairs. Then they'd said goodnight, and she had gone upstairs too.

Pollard raised a quizzical eyebrow.

'Rather a protracted goodnight?' he suggested.

'I'm afraid it was. I just can't imagine what we should do if Mrs Makepeace left. It would be a catastrophe for the school...as a matter of fact I've been worrying about it ever since.'

'Still, if her personal happiness is involved...I'm sure Inspector Toye would take this view. He's a romantic, you know.'

Toye, seated with his notebook at one of the library tables, directed a look of reproach at his superior officer, and waited with pen ostentatiously poised.

'I suppose Mr Jay and Mrs Makepeace were too absorbed to notice the light in your office,' Pollard pursued. 'There are glass panels in the door, aren't there?'

'Damn it, I hadn't put the light on,' Andrew Medlicott burst out violently. 'All right, I'll explain. I'm sure you're thinking it's fishy that I kept noticing the time. You'll think I'm round the bend, I expect. Perhaps I am.'

'I see no symptoms of it whatever. Did you perhaps feel that people might let their hair down as it was the last night, and that you'd better keep an unobtrusive eye on things?'

'That's exactly what I did feel,' Andrew Medlicott replied with quick gratitude. 'It's a frightful responsibility, you know, being in charge of this great barrack of a place during the holidays. The Governors just don't begin to understand what's involved. One cigarette end dropped in the common rooms that night, and the whole building would have gone up...I decided to lie low until everybody had gone to bed, and then do a round.'

127

'They're very lucky to have a chap with your standards of responsibility on the job. Could you carry on with telling us anything else you heard or saw? It might be really important.'

'Well, the next thing that happened was that Boothby came back.'

'What time was that?'

'Twenty-five to eleven. My watch has a luminous dial, and I kept looking at it, and wishing the time would go faster, so that I could get home. Boothby sat in his car for a few minutes. Then he came in, and behaved rather oddly, I thought. He came straight in here, actually, didn't put the light on, and sat down in the window. I—er—shifted that hatch affair you can see over there just a crack, and could see him quite clearly, as the porch light shines in. Once he gave a sort of groan, and kept looking round. Then after about ten minutes he got up and went out into the hall. I looked out through my door, and saw him going upstairs— to bed—I suppose. He—'

Andrew Medlicott broke off abruptly and stared at Pollard, horror-struck.

'He hadn't—hadn't just?—'

'No,' Pollard replied emphatically. 'You can put that idea right out of your head. Boothby is not Wendy Shaw's murderer.'

'Thank God for that anyway. It would have been the end from the school's point of view, seeing that he was based here. Think of the publicity...Well, not long after Boothby cleared off, the racket down in the common rooms stopped, and people started drifting along to the entrance hall, and going upstairs. By about ten past the party which had been to the King William had come back, and everything was quiet. I could hear Jay doing a round himself. Now he's an awfully decent responsible chap. If he hadn't been in charge, I should have been much more worried about the Fort-night.'

'And then?' Pollard prompted.

'As soon as Jay had gone past, and down the corridor to the classroom he used as an office, and I'd heard him shut the door, I—er—took off my shoes and went around myself. You know, cigarette ends, TV plugs left in, and whatever. Everything was all right, actually. Then I pushed off home. It was a vile night, raining cats and dogs, and blowing half a gale, so any noise I made when I went out was drowned by it all.'

'Did you meet anybody on the way home?'

'Not a soul. Wait a bit, though. A car was coming from the Biddle Bay direction as I came out of the drive. It was just on the half-hour when I got in, as my wife would tell you. As a matter of fact I think I can hear her arriving with the car to pick me up. We're going into Winnage. Er—I don't want her to know what I've just told you. She thought I'd stayed on for the party, you see.'

'Quite,' Pollard replied reassuringly. 'There's no need to mention it.'

Daphne Medlicott, ushered into the library by Toye, impressed Pollard favourably. Sympathetic but sensible, he thought, and pleasant to look at, if not a beauty. IQ nothing out of the way, but gives you a feeling of security. Just the type for Medlicott, poor chap.

'We liked the Horner staff so much,' she was saying. 'The Kings, especially, because of the birdwatching. Andrew's got quite keen since we moved down here. They invited us to join an expedition to a marvellous colony of ravens, in a most ungetatable place beyond Starbury, and to see the Fortnight Film, too. I was furious at missing it, but I'd developed a streaming cold, and it really didn't seem fair to go.'

'I don't suppose you saw or heard anything unusual on the road outside your house while you were alone that evening?' Pollard asked.

Daphne Medlicott shook her head.

'Nothing at all. I went to bed early, and read until Andrew came in about half-past eleven, and remember thinking how little traffic there was.'

'Even the Fortnight Film wouldn't have got me out on a night like that,' her husband commented. 'It was one of King's bird films which they put on first that lured me down here.'

'This terrible business,' Daphne said, turning to Pollard. 'Do you think it is likely to do the school permanent harm?

I shouldn't have expected it to, myself, but my husband is very anxious about it.'

'Have there been any withdrawals by parents?' Pollard asked.

'Only one, actually,' Andrew Medlicott admitted, 'but it's early days yet.'

'I don't think you're likely to get many more, then. People who panic and rush into action usually do it at once.'

Daphne beamed at him.

'That's so reassuring. How would you have felt if your daughter had been at school here?'

Pollard conjured up a mental picture of Rose in a diminutive school uniform, complete with hat and badge.

'I'd know, alas, that you can't guarantee freedom from violent crime anywhere these days,' he told her.

Shortly after this the Medlicotts went off.

'Well,' Pollard said, subsiding on to the library window seat, 'bang goes Medlicott, taking Boothby with him. Thanks to Aunt Is, we know very well that Stubbs must be counted out, even if we haven't finally checked up on him yet. 'We're left with Don Glover, and the soul-searing prospect of starting from scratch.'

He stared out of the window at people disporting themselves happily on the crowded beach below.

'You handled Mr Medlicott a treat,' Toye remarked after a pause.

'Poor blighter! Temperamentally doomed to become a rat race casualty. Well, let's be thankful we've got jobs, even if we don't seem to be making much of them at the moment. We'd better hoist ourselves up, and call at Uncharted Seas before lunch. You know, I've got a hunch that Glover *was* heading there when Stubbs saw him pass the King William that Friday night.'

'Meaning that he either couldn't get an answer when he arrived and went back home as he says, or—'

'Or he did the job. There'd have been plenty of time before the Stoneham party got back. Even if the train was dead on time they couldn't have turned up before half past eleven at the earliest. Come on, we must step on it. The Horner lunch will be getting under way.'

Once again, Eddy Horner opened the front door to them himself. He gave them a sharp interrogative look.

'I'm afraid we've no definite news for you, Mr Horner,' Pollard told him, 'but that doesn't mean that quite a lot of progress hasn't been made since we were here last. Can you spare a few minutes?'

As they sat down in the long sitting room with its superb view out to sea, he sensed a change of atmosphere. This time Eddy Horner seemed preoccupied rather than almost crushed by the disaster, and there was a litter of papers on the desk, as if some sorting operation were in progress. Coming straight to the point, Pollard asked if the trip to Stoneham on Friday nights had been a regular fixture for some time.

'Since Penny and the baby came down at the end of June, my son-in-law's been down every weekend but two, counting this one,' Eddy Horner told him.

'So it could be known locally that Wendy was very likely to be alone here for several hours on a Friday evening?'

'Penny and I didn't always both go. Here, she'd better come in on this.'

In response to a shout from her father Penny Townsend appeared from the guest wing. Pretty and smartly turned out as before, she also struck Pollard as distraite. After some argument a desk diary was produced, and it was agreed that seven trips in all had been made to Stoneham, on five of which she had accompanied her father.

'So that anyone knowing that Mrs Townsend was still staying here could have banked on a strong probability of your both being out on the evening of Wendy's death?' Pollard summarized.

'That's correct,' Eddy Horner replied.

'Would you say that your comings and goings are known to a fairly wide circle of people?'

'No, I wouldn't. For one thing, I don't go in for much social life locally, and for another we're a bit off the map up here. A few friends would know, and Mrs Barrow might have said something about it in the village, I suppose.'

Penny Townsend, who had been listening to the conversation with barely concealed impatience, suddenly came in.

'All the people who were here for drinks the night before

the Fortnight started would know, Dad. I remember you saying what a shame it was that it was the only weekend Bob couldn't make it.'

'Who was at this party?' Pollard asked.

'Oh, the Fortnight staff. Mrs Makepeace, the housekeeper at the school, and their bursar and his wife. Wendy, of course …that's all, I think. Oh, and Don Glover barged in at half-time—uninvited. I can't do with that guy.'

'Chap oversells himself,' her father conceded, 'but he knows his way round in business. But I recall he didn't turn up until after we'd been talking about Bob coming down. The doorbell broke into it.'

'I'd like to go on to another matter now,' Pollard said. 'Even though you didn't find anything disturbed when you came back from Stoneham on August 20, the most obvious explanation for Wendy's murder remains that she surprised a thief. What was there in the way of valuables and cash in the place that night?'

'Nothing that a professional crook would have been interested in,' Eddy Horner replied. 'That's what's so damn baffling about the business. The silver I've got down here doesn't add up to a hill of beans, and I don't go in for Old Masters or first editions or whatever. Nor do I keep much cash in the place. There might have been fifty quid in a drawer in my desk—not more.'

'What about you, Mrs Townsend?' Pollard asked.

'Not more than ten pounds or so in cash,' she said. 'I'd got the rest on me. And I was wearing my rings, and a rather valuable diamond pendant. The brooches and earrings in my dressing table drawer wouldn't be worth more than a couple of hundred at the outside.'

'Murders have been committed for far less than the amounts that have been mentioned, you know. And there are other things that a certain type of thief is interested in,' Pollard went on. 'Mr Horner, did you have any business papers here that might have been of importance to a competitor, we'll say?'

Eddy Horner looked up sharply.

'I hadn't thought of that one,' he admitted. 'There were

132

some confidential papers about a possible deal, but nothing on a scale to attract a break-in.'

'I expect you're wondering what all this is leading up to. I'll tell you. From information received, it seems highly probable that someone called here on the night of Wendy's murder. As you say, your close friends wouldn't have expected to find you at home. It was late for a social call from a casual acquaintance, and not the sort of night when most people would choose to be out. Can you think of anyone who might have wanted to see you urgently on business?'

There was a slight sound from Penny Townsend's direction. Eddy Horner, who had been lying back in his chair with his hands in his pockets, looked up; and Pollard once again sensed the little man's formidable quality.

'Nobody at all,' he replied tersely.

'Thank you,' Pollard said. 'I think that's all I need bother you about at the moment.'

Toye put away his notebook, and escorted by a monosyllabic Eddy Horner they made their way to the front door, Penny Townsend having vanished on some murmured pretext. As the car moved off Pollard told Toye to drive to the King William.

'I swear Glover comes into this somehow,' he said. 'Unless I'm very much mistaken, Horner will make for his place after lunch. He's got to pass the pub to get there. We'll give the party time to get going, and then go along and gatecrash.

They managed to park with a clear view of the road, and took it in turns to go into the King William for a snack. Then, Pollard having successfully got it across to Jack Nancekivell that they were visiting the pub incognito, they settled down in their car to wait.

'If Glover did go up there that night, do you take it that there's some deal on between him and Horner?' Toye asked.

'Yes, and I'll make a guess at what it is. My aunt told me that rumours are going round that Glover's trying to get hold of the land above his caravan site for expansion. Perhaps he's thinking big, and trying to get Horner to come in on it.'

'But if it was as urgent as all that, you'd think he'd have rung Horner first thing on Saturday morning, and said he'd called there the night before.'

'No, I don't think he would,' Pollard said thoughtfully. 'The news that Wendy Shaw was missing would have been all over Kittitoe by breakfast time—you know what village grapevines are like, and Glover might very well have felt it wiser to lie low about his call. Quite apart from any deal, he's desperately keen to be in with the local leading lights. But there's another explanation, of course.'

'That Wendy looked out, saw the caller wasn't Boothby, opened the door to Glover and got strangled for her pains?'

'Just that. You weren't as well placed as I was to see Horner's reaction when I suggested that someone had come on business, but the way he clammed up stood out a mile, didn't it? I'm convinced that his mind went straight to Glover, and he saw the red light. Quite apart from his feelings about Wendy, he'd see the headlines—you know. Travel Firm Tycoon in Deal with Killer of his Female Relative. If I'm right, there's going to be one hell of a confrontation shortly. What's the time?'

Soon after two there was a cheerful exodus from the pub, and the sound of a door being slammed and locked. The car park emptied rapidly, and before long the police car was the only occupant. The minutes slipped away, and Pollard began to get anxious, and consider alternative courses of action.

'We'll hang on a bit longer, and then find another stance,' he said. 'We stick out like a sore thumb alone here. I wonder—'

He broke off as a Jaguar suddenly appeared from the direction of Biddle Bay. Toye exclaimed with admiration as it swept silently past at controlled speed.

'A real beaut,' he said gloatingly. 'How long do we give him, sir?'

'Say five minutes. If he's really going to Glover's, I want them to be in it up to the neck before we show up.'

The Glover house was about half a mile beyond Kittitoe on the Winnage road. As they turned in at the gate, Pollard visibly relaxed at the sight of the Jaguar parked behind the white Ford Capri.

'Hand it to you, sir,' Toye remarked.

They got out of the car, and walked on the grass verge

134

of the drive towards the house, a solid Edwardian affair in red brick with two preposterous pepperbox turrets. As they came up to it, angry voices could be heard through an open window.

'Our arrivals are getting monotonous, aren't they?' Pollard murmured in Toye's ear.

Unnoticed they walked through the open front door into the hall. A woman who was unashamedly listening outside a closed door turned sharply. She was small and round-faced, with straight faded fair hair which was parted in the centre and taken back into a bun. She wore a well-cut brown linen frock which she made look dowdy. Ageless type, Pollard thought, consigning her tentatively to the early fifties.

'Mrs Glover?' he asked politely. 'Good afternoon. I'm Detective-Superintendent Pollard of New Scotland Yard. Could I have a word with your husband?'

He saw that she was poised to spring to his defence, but precisely at this moment Don Glover's voice bellowed from behind the closed door.

'Go on! Say it! Say you think I murdered the girl!'

Apparently deciding that Scotland Yard was less of a menace than the enemy within, she flung open the door.

'Police,' she announced tersely, and darting into the room stationed herself beside her husband.

Pollard and Toye followed her. Don Glover in shirtsleeves, burly and blazing, confronted a poker-faced Eddy Horner across the dining room table.

'I'll have the law on the whole lot of you,' Don Glover shouted.

'I represent the law, you know,' Pollard remarked conversationally. 'Shall we sit down?'

The temperature took a sudden nosedive. In silence the party seated itself round the highly polished mahogany table, in the centre of which a vase of marigolds stood on an oval embroidered mat.

'I'm sure,' Pollard said, 'that I needn't tell either of you two gentlemen that you are entitled to refuse to answer any of my questions except in the presence of a solicitor.'

'I don't want a bloody solicitor,' Don Glover replied. 'I've nothing to hide.'

'I'm quite capable of protecting my own interests, thank you,' Eddy Horner said coldly.

'Right. Well, Mr Glover, where did you spend the evening of Friday, August 20, between eight and ten-forty-five pm?'

Don Glover stared at him.

'Having dinner at the Crown in Winnage most of the time.'

'Were you dining alone?'

'No. I was with a chap called Basil Thornhurst. He's the Area Planning Officer, if you must know.'

'Indeed I must. It's important, from your point of view as well as mine. I'm going to put it to you that on August 20 you were granted planning permission to develop the fields above your caravan site as a residential holiday area of some kind.'

There was a stupified silence. Don Glover's mouth fell slightly open. A glint of reluctant admiration appeared in Eddy Horner's eyes.

'As you don't contradict me, I take it that I'm right,' Pollard continued. 'I rather think you felt that, given Mr Horner's financial backing, the area as a whole had far-reaching possibilities. And being a man who doesn't let the grass grow under his feet, I think that after you got back here from your dinner you drove over to Uncharted Seas to put the scheme to him, arriving there at about ten-thirty.'

'S'right,' Don Glover said hoarsely.

'What I'm interested in, Mr Glover, is when you arrived back here again. In your statement the other day you said it must have been about a quarter to eleven. Can you produce a witness of this, preferably other than Mrs Glover?'

Don Glover stared helplessly at his wife.

'Of course you can, you great booby,' she exploded with the fury of the badly frightened. 'Reverend Fuller was on the phone as you came in at the door, about the Sunday evening service at the Site, and you took over from me. You weren't gone above quarter of an hour to twenty minutes.'

'My God, you're right,' her husband almost whispered. 'I'd clean forgotten. Not that he'll remember the time, I don't suppose.'

'May we use your telephone?' Pollard asked. 'Toye, ring the vicarage, and if the vicar's in, ask him if he'd come here

136

for five minutes. You can run down for him.'

'Why the hell didn't you say you'd been over to the bungalow that Friday night, Glover, and save all this hullabaloo?' Eddy Horner demanded indignantly after Toye had gone out.

'I didn't contact you over the weekend because any fool would know that you wouldn't want to be bothered, with the girl missing,' Don Glover told him. 'Then once the murder was out, well, I wasn't going to look for trouble.'

'Withholding information from the police invariably leads to trouble, you know,' Pollard remarked.

An uneasy silence descended, finally broken by Mrs Glover.

'I'll get the kettle on,' she said. 'The Reverend can do with a cuppa anytime, and I daresay one wouldn't do any of us harm.'

Eddy Horner mechanically opened the door for her, and she scurried out, embarrassed.

Pollard turned to Don Glover, who had recovered most of his normal self-assurance, but kept eyeing Eddy Horner.

'What happened when you arrived at Uncharted Seas that night?' he asked.

'Nothing. I rang, and nobody came. I could hear the telly going, and thought they hadn't heard the ring, so I had another go, and after that I hammered on the door. In the end I decided that they must be out, and had told the little girl not to open the door to anyone, so I got into the car and came back home, hoping I hadn't scared her.'

Eddy Horner moved abruptly in his chair.

'Owe you an apology, Glover. I shouldn't have taken the line I did. Truth is, I'm not as young as I was, and this business of Wendy has knocked me for six. Hope our deal's still on,' he added with an appraising glance.

Clever old devil, thought Pollard...quite a psychologist.

Don Glover came slightly larger than life.

'Forget it, Horner. I'd've gone a lot further in your shoes. As to the deal, it can't go through too soon for me.'

'That's fine. It can't for me, either. I'm clearing out of Kittitoe. Putting the bungalow on the market.'

'Clearing out?' Don Glover echoed in dismay.

'Yea. I'll never find another place to touch Uncharted Seas, but after what happened I can't get Beckon Cove out of my mind, day or night. It's haunting me, you can say if you like. Care to buy the property yourself? At a professional valuation, of course,' Eddy Horner added hastily.

Into Don Glover's face came the incredulous expression of a man who sees undreamt-of bliss suddenly within his grasp. He opened his mouth to reply, then checked himself.

'I'd like to talk it over with the wife,' he said, as a car drew up outside the window.

The Reverend Arthur Fuller, vicar of Kittitoe, suggested a puffin. His nose was parrotty, his gait waddling, and as he came in a pair of shrewd eyes briefly engaged Pollard's. He evinced no surprise at his urgent summons, nor at the company present, and listened politely to an explanation of the Yard's policy of getting confirmation of all statements made during a murder investigation.

'Ah, yes,' he said, from the chair at the head of the table, into which he had been ushered by tacit consent. 'Fortunately I can be of some assistance here. On the night in question I rang Mr Glover about a service on the caravan site, at just before twenty minutes to eleven.'

'How is it that you can be so sure of the time, sir?' Pollard asked.

'Because one of my favourite radio programmes was starting at a quarter to eleven, Superintendent—a serial reading. They're doing George Eliot's *Scenes from Clerical Life*, you know. Entirely delightful. I wonder if any of you are following it?'

At this juncture the appearance of Mrs Glover with a tea-tray produced in Pollard the sensation of taking part in a drawing room comedy. As the cups circulated, it transpired that no one, himself included, was familiar with *Scenes from Clerical Life*, but Toye unexpectedly came into his own, having followed *Adam Bede* in twelve instalments during a period of sick leave. Eddy Horner and Don Glover detached themselves from this literary conversation, and began to discuss demolition costs, in connection, Pollard hoped, with the existing caravan site. Left to entertain Mrs Glover, he fell back on the infallible interest topic of the twins.

138

Later, they dropped Arthur Fuller, discreet to the last, at the vicarage.

'Well, there seem to be just three bits of formal checking-up between us and Square One,' Pollard remarked, as they went on. 'There's the Planning bloke, the radio programmes for August 20, and where Stubbs was during the early part of the evening. We'd better make for Pike's place.'

They found Constable Pike triumphant to the point of garrulity.

'Mr Stubbs was at home all right on the Friday night, sir,' he told Pollard. 'There was a lady called at the house, and she saw him, although she was in the kitchen most of the time between quarter to nine and quarter to ten, having a tell with Mrs Stubbs. She'd got behind with her delivery of free range eggs because of trouble with her van, else she wouldn't have been so late. She's on the WI committee, like Mrs Stubbs, my wife says. It was my wife remembered that she'd come here very late that night, and why 'twas. I thought the Stubbs would have free range for sure, so I went up there—to Miss Honeybun's place, I mean—this afternoon, and got a statement from her.'

'Go back to the beginning on an egg,' Pollard commented.

'Sir?' Pike looked baffled.

'I'm only thinking of where all this lands us, Pike. You've done extremely well, and I'll see that the management knows about it. And congratulations to Mrs Pike, too, for her bit of help. We must be getting back to Stoneham now.'

When they were clear of the village he turned to Toye.

'Do you know,' he said, 'I think our best hope is to go home, and take a day off tomorrow to clear our heads. Then buckle down to the file again. We'll go up on the midnight train.'

12

Eureka !
Attributed to Archimedes
in his bath.

Arriving at Paddington in the small hours, Pollard slept briefly at the Yard before returning to his home at Wimbledon for breakfast. He let himself into the house very quietly against a voluble chorus from the kitchen. For a couple of seconds he stood observing the scene unnoticed. His son and daughter in little blue boiler suits sat on either side of their mother, dividing their attention between their cereal bowls and urgent communication with her. Jane, also in blue, was engaged in a complex operation of listening, responding, inculcating the rudiments of civilized eating, and consuming her own breakfast. Three red-gold heads formed the highlights of the picture. Then Jane looked up, suddenly sensing his presence.

'I'll knock you up bacon and eggs in a brace of shakes,' she said, when the tumult of excitement had died down. 'Get them on to the next stage, will you?'

Later in the meal he announced that he was up against a brick wall, and had come home for a day off.

'Super!' she exclaimed. 'The Blakes brought me fifty pounds of plums from Evesham yesterday. Now I can jam and bottle in a big way, while you take over the twins.'

'Here,' Pollard protested, looking round for the au pair. 'Where's Gianna?'

'It's her day off. You're definitely for it. Just what you

need to keep your mind off the case: you won't be able to hear yourself think.'

In the event, strenuous nursemaiding all the morning followed by sleep in a garden chair during the afternoon proved an effective anaesthetic. It was not until the twins were bedded down, and supper had been eaten and cleared away that he found his thoughts drifting back irresistibly towards Kittitoe.

'Yes, I think it might help to put the whole thing into narrative form,' he replied in response to a suggestion from Jane. 'I'll just set out the facts without looking them in the face, so to speak.'

In a leisurely way, with frequent pauses, he filled in the complex background of the case, and gave her thumbnail character sketches of the dramatis personae. Finally he summarised the course of events. When he came to an end, Jane, who had been completely absorbed, put down her needlework.

'You do put things over well,' she remarked. 'You've made all these people with their preoccupations and obsessions and what-have-you really come alive to me.'

'You're a good listener: it's a rare gift.'

Pollard stretched, and recrossed his long legs, clasping his hands behind his head, a favourite attitude when he was wrestling with a problem.

'If one of them is Wendy Shaw's murderer,' he said after a pause, 'then he's got preoccupations and obsessions I haven't begun to discover. If she was killed by a complete outsider, well, God help us. There were masses of people staying in and around Kittitoe. Take Biddle Bay to begin with: it's a much bigger place, bung full of hotels and boarding houses.'

'You haven't touched on motive.'

'The only viable suggestion here seems to be that she was either killed by a psychopath or surprised a break-in. Plenty of robbery with violence blokes around, and quite a few psychopaths unfortunately. There isn't much of a lead there, I'm afraid.'

'We have been here before, you know,' Jane said. 'Up against a brick wall, I mean.'

141

'True.' Pollard poured himself out some more beer, and raised his glass to her. 'Here's hoping.'

On the following morning Pollard woke with a sentence clearly formulated in his mind...Wendy Shaw had no known contacts of importance in Kittitoe except Geoff Boothby, who's out...Surprised, he began to evaluate it, but almost at once the alarm of the Teamaker went off, and Jane, a quick waker, was sitting up in bed. On a sudden impulse he decided to keep his waking thought to himself for the present. Discussing it in the turmoil of getting the household launched on another day might somehow blur it, he felt.

His date with Toye at the Yard was for eleven, but he arrived an hour early to do some thinking on his own. After saying that he did not want to be disturbed, he settled down at his desk, wrote the sentence on a sheet of paper, and propped it up in front of him. Then lighting a cigarette, he leant back in his chair to consider it at leisure.

Penny Townsend had been emphatic about Wendy's reluctance to go out and about in Kittitoe before the alleged girl friend, actually Geoff Boothby, turned up. Therefore unknown contacts in the place could be ruled out. Suppose a psychopath, either a resident or a holidaymaker, had spotted Wendy, marked her down, and managed to find out that she was going to be alone in the bungalow on the evening of 20 August. Pollard came to the conclusion that, although improbable, this hypothesis could not be entirely ruled out. But a far more convincing one was that her murder was unpremeditated, and incidental to attempted robbery. But thinking on this line brought one up against formidable difficulties.

He drew on his cigarette, frowning deeply. Of course a break-in would have been easy enough. Even if the garden door had not carelessly been left unlocked, there were the windows. These were casements, he had noticed, and it seemed unlikely that all the top lights had been secured. Besides, it was a noisy night of wind and rain and a rough sea. The careful breaking of a pane of glass well away from the telly in the sitting room would have been a simple matter.

OK, Pollard thought, fine, but from here on it just doesn't make sense. You're landed with two types of housebreaker, and neither adds up. There's the small chap who's been keeping an eye on the place, and hopes to pick up any cash and jewellery that he can get his hands on. If surprised in the act he might knock someone out, but the idea of him strangling a defenceless girl, dumping her body in the sea, and clearing off without leaving the least sign of disturbance is fantastic. Or there's the big chap, except that he wouldn't come unless there was something removable which made the job worth while, and old Horner declares there wasn't. And anyway, that type shoots its way out if cornered, and strangling's an improvised sort of murder. Hell, I've been over all this a dozen times, and got nowhere...

Pollard shifted his position restlessly, and made a fresh cast. Taking the timetable of the events of the night of 20 August out of the file, he inserted the recently gathered information about Hugh Stubbs, Don Glover and Andrew Medlicott. The one thing that emerged from these additions was that it seemed highly probable that the murder was committed earlier rather than later. Between approximately 9.50 pm and 10.30 pm Geoff Boothby and Don Glover had both rung and knocked in vain, and Eddy Horner's telephone call had been unanswered. Of course, there was the period between Don Glover's departure and the return of the Horner-Townsend trio at 11.40 pm, about which there was no evidence in regard to the bungalow, but the earlier silence was very suggestive, and the PM report had said the body was in the water for 'at least' forty-eight hours.

Presently abandoning the timetable, he fell to staring at the sentence propped up in front of him, idly shifting the emphasis from word to word... Wendy Shaw had NO known contacts of importance...no CONTACTS of importance... no contacts of IMPORTANCE...

At this point his flagging interest was alerted. Had Wendy unimportant, perhaps trifling, contacts which turned out in the course of events to be highly significant? Pollard shut his eyes, and thought hard. The people who came in for drinks when she was a dead loss socially according to that bitchy little Penny Townsend? He was just making a note to enquire into their identities when he also remembered the drinks party on the eve of the Kittitoe Fortnight. He checked his memory by referring to the file, and made a hasty list. Rule out the women, and you were left with five men: Boothby, Glover and Medlicott, all cleared, Jay and King.

He crossed off the first three. Jay...hardly, but he must check the time at which Marcia Makepeace joined him in the gallery at the film show. King...

After a timeless interval Pollard found himself surfacing, his pen still poised over Paul King's name. Slowly and deliberately he put the pen down and sat motionless, reviewing the events of the evening of Wendy Shaw's murder.

First of all, a late return from the expedition had thrown out the schedule for the rest of the day. On his own statement, supported by that of others, King had gone to the lab he was using as a dark room to finish editing the Fortnight Film, emerging for dinner, and after a further disappearance finally arriving in the assembly hall with the finished film at about 8.40 pm. This last time would be easily verifiable. In the meantime Eddy Horner and his daughter had left for Stoneham at about seven o'clock, and Wendy had spoken to Aunt Is on the phone at eight.

Much more exact timing was wanted for some of this, Pollard thought, tugging absently at his hair. When did dinner begin and end, for instance? How did King go to Uncharted Seas, if he were the murderer? On foot or by car? If the latter, he must surely have borrowed one without the owner subsequently discovering this: the dormobile was so conspicuous. Risky—much more likely that he went on foot, shinning up the bank near the drive gate to avoid going out into the road at all. But if he went and returned on foot, he must have left Uncharted Seas quite by 8.25 pm to get to the assembly hall by 8.40 pm.

Pollard's mind flashed back to the timing of dinner that night. Another reason for seeing Marcia Makepeace. She had said that she was driving up to London today, Sunday, and had given him her address and telephone number. Too early to ring her, though. She'd hardly make it before midday.

After the recent period of stalemate he found himself being swept along in a positive torrent of ideas. The film editing, for instance. Had this been a pretext to account for King's absence between dinner and 8.40 pm? Could the editing have been done beforehand, during the night, perhaps? Pollard had a vivid mental picture of the door at the rear of the school building, so handy for the labs and the Kings' dormobile, parked where they could be sure of privacy, as Michael Jay had said...Of course, if there'd been any funny business of this sort, Janice King was in it up to the neck...

At this point another idea forcibly presented itself. If the film editing was bogus, it had been made to appear wholly convincing by the late return from the expedition. Had this been engineered in some way? If it could be proved that King had staged a hold-up, this would be conclusive evidence that he was planning something illegal. The firm supplying the coaches must be contacted, and Marcia Makepeace would know the name and address: she must be got hold of at the earliest possible moment.

As Pollard scribbled hastily on a desk pad, the door opened quietly to admit Toye, as always impeccably neat and dead on time.

'Don't start chucking your hat in the air,' Pollard told him, 'but it's possible we're on to something. Come and sit down, and I'll tell you.'

By the time the ground had been covered Toye was showing barely suppressed excitement.

'Fits like a glove,' he said. 'Start to finish.'

'Here, easy,' Pollard said. 'Don't get carried away. I admit that the details look quite convincing, but the whole thing doesn't fit together, you know.'

'I don't think I'm with you, sir.'

'I mean that it looks as though King could have engineered cover for a visit to Uncharted Seas all right, but what made all the scheming worth while, not to mention bumping off Wendy Shaw? We've found a way through one brick wall only to come slap up against another. However, we'd better concentrate on circumstantial evidence at the moment. The Kings themselves, to start with: past history, present affairs, especially financial—the lot. It *would* be a Bank Holiday weekend, but enquiries could get off the ground. You can set all this in train.'

'Then there's the coach hire firm,' Toye suggested.

'Yes. I swear that muddle over the time for starting back on August 20 stinks somehow. We want Mrs Makepeace for the firm's name. Then there's the business of the film editing. I'm a bit out of my depth here. Do you run a ciné camera?'

'Not on my pay, sir.'

Pollard flicked a switch.

'Is Sergeant Boyce on today?' he asked. 'If so, get him along here, will you?'

'I'll find out, sir,' a disembodied voice replied.

In a couple of minutes it announced that Sergeant Boyce was reporting immediately, and a couple more saw the arrival of the photographer of Pollard's team. Boyce was a cheerful six-footer with fingers permanently stained with chemicals, and hair long to the limit of permissibility.

'Good,' Pollard said. 'I'm glad you were around. I want some technical information which I ought to possess already. Better to keep one's ignorance in the family.'

Boyce grinned broadly.

'Shoot, sir,' he invited, 'And I'll do my best.'

Pollard folded his arms and rested them on his desk.

'Take a semi-professional photographer attached to a travel firm,' he said. 'Part of his job is to film the activities of what I believe they call special interest holidays, and show the result at the end. Would a chap of this type be capable of processing his film?'

'Easily, sir, especially if it was black and white.'

'How long does processing take?'

'About an hour and a half. Then the film's got to dry off — probably less for that.'

'When it's dry, I take it you don't bung it into a projector, and show it just as it is?'

'Not as a general rule, you wouldn't. Not if it was a public showing, anyway. It's got to be edited, you see.'

'This is what Inspector Toye and I are not clear about,' Pollard said, 'so let's have it in words of one syllable.'

'Well, sir,' Boyce replied, 'however nifty you are with a ciné camera, you'll have some poorish shots which you'll want to cut out, or too many of the same subject. Then you'll almost certainly want to do a bit of regrouping: have all the shots of the kids or the garden consecutive. You probably took them on different days, and filmed other subjects in between. All this means cutting the film, arranging the bits in another order, and splicing them with transparent adhesive tape. The combined ops are called editing.'

'Finicky sort of job,' Toye remarked.

'It's finicky, all right—takes hours. You want plenty of space, and a lot of spare reels to wind the bits you aren't using on, especially if you're dealing with several films at once, as your chap must have been.'

Pollard sat plunged in thought.

'Well, thanks, Boyce,' he said at last. 'I've got the hang of it all now, although I can't see exactly where it leads yet. I'll probably be coming back.'

After Boyce had gone Pollard and Toye spent a few minutes drawing up a course of action. Then Toye departed to set going the enquiries about the Kings, and Pollard dialled the London telephone number which Marcia Makepeace had given him. To his surprise and gratification she answered in person.

'I got off early,' she explained, 'before the traffic built up.'

On being asked if she could face a visit to the Yard, she replied that she was not in the least tired, and would gladly come if she could be of any help.

'I expect you're just going to have some lunch,' Pollard said. 'Suppose we send a car for you at half-past two?'

This being settled, he went off to get some lunch himself.

Afterwards, while sorting out his points for discussion with Marcia, he re-read Paul King's statements at Crowncliff in the light of Boyce's information about film editing.

The Fortnight Film must have been quite a lengthy affair, he mused, quite a number of ciné films having gone to its making, and a lot of editing would have been needed to have made a coherent record of all the various ploys. King had presumably processed and edited as he went along. He had claimed to be dealing with the final film on the evening of August 20, the one which he had intended to process on Thursday night, and partly edit on Friday morning, completing its integration into the Fortnight Film as a whole after returning from the expedition on Friday afternoon. Had he actually done the whole job during Thursday night? Although sleeping in their dormobile, the Kings must have had access to the school building during the night, for bathrooms and loos. On the other hand there was the possibility of an old film being used...

Marcia Makepeace's arrival broke in on his thoughts. As Toye ushered her into the room Pollard was once again struck by her air of confident happiness. Attractive, he thought, and so likeable, taking in her good figure and fine eyes, wide-set and steady in their gaze.

'It's good of you to come so promptly,' he told her. 'I won't keep you long. Just a few points about times, to begin with. What time was dinner at St Julitta's on the last night—August 20, that is?'

'At seven o'clock, just as usual.'

'Can you remember how long the meal took?'

'Yes, I can,' she replied. 'A bit longer than usual, as it was a special effort to finish up with. The actual service of the meal was over by twenty to eight, but there were a few speeches and presentations after that. The dining room wasn't clear of people until about five to eight.'

'I expect timing is a problem with non-resident staff, isn't it?'

'It certainly is. There are overtime rates, for one thing, and quite apart from that, most of my women are married, and one doesn't want to disrupt what home life they have.'

'Did anyone go out of dinner early?' Pollard asked as casually as he could.

'Only Paul King, to finish editing the Fortnight Film. He'd said he'd have to cut the speeches.'

Pollard moved on quickly to the subject of the coaches. Here Marcia told him that she could not understand how the muddle about the time of return had arisen.

'I'm not really clear about what actually happened,' she said. 'As you can imagine, everyone was a bit het up when they did get back, and there wasn't time to go into it. But I can only say that Wright of Biddle Bay is a most reliable firm. The school always uses them for matches and outings, so I can speak from experience. I've never known them make a bish before. And Michael Jay is terrifically competent, and

I can't believe that he slipped up over the arrangements. He was very put out by the hitch,' she added, amused by the recollection.

'Now one more thing,' Pollard said. 'I think you and Mr Jay watched the film show from the gallery, didn't you?'

'Yes, we did.'

'Can you tell me just when the Fortnight Film started? A shorter one was shown first, I believe?'

'Yes, one of Paul King's lovely bird films, to fill in time until he'd got the main one ready. I came in about half-past eight when I'd had my dinner, and saw the last bit of it. The Fortnight Film started amid cheers at ten to nine. I was clock-conscious because of my staff.'

Toye was making shorthand notes of the interview, but Pollard made a show of writing himself while considering his next approach.

'I know very little about ciné films,' he said conversationally. 'My wife and I only rise to colour transparencies. Why did there have to be this last-minute work on the Fortnight Film?'

'Because without editing it would have been so bitty. All sorts of activities had been going on, and had been shot just as they happened. It made much better sense if—say everything to do with botany—was grouped together.'

'I see,' Pollard replied. 'And I suppose the last film would have been the final stages of the work done, and simply had to be included?'

'Oh, yes. The main thing on it was the expedition to Winnage on the Thursday, which summed up Michael's course on settlement. I went on it, actually, and it was simply fascinating. I'd no idea what an interesting town Winnage is, both historically and architecturally.'

'Did you feature in the film?' Pollard asked, smiling at her.

'I did, as a matter of fact. Several of the Fortnighters were in it, too. We were only lay figures against important backgrounds, though.'

So it wasn't simply a film from a previous year, Pollard thought...

'Well, the Kittitoe Fortnight seems to have been highly successful,' he said aloud. 'I wonder how the one at Crown-

149

cliff has gone? It ends tomorrow night, doesn't it?'

'Yes, it does.' Marcia looked suddenly radiant. 'I'll be hearing all about it from Michael on Tuesday evening.' Her eyes met Pollard's. 'We're going to be married, you know. I don't know why I'm telling you this,' she added, going pink.

'It's charming of you to tell us,' Pollard said warmly, 'isn't it, Toye? We aren't often told anything as nice as this in our rather sordid job. May I wish you both great happiness?'

Toye, overcome by the occasion, took refuge in formality, and wished to be associated with what the Superintendent had said.

'When is the wedding to be?' Pollard asked.

'Oh, not until the New Year. I have to give St Julitta's a term's notice—it's in my contract, and anyway, I wouldn't leave them in the lurch. You know,' she hesitated a little, 'I can't help feeling a bit guilty at being so happy. This ghastly business about Wendy, and all the misery and worry it's causing people...'

'You mustn't dwell on it,' Pollard told her. 'You were only involved in it incidentally. Don't let it spoil your happiness.'

'Thank you,' she said, as they both got to their feet, 'that's helped.'

He watched her go out of the room with Toye in attendance, and immediately sat down at his desk, grabbed a sheet of paper and began to make notes.

After a short time Toye reappeared, having arranged transport for Marcia.

'All starry-eyed, aren't you?' remarked Pollard, glancing up at him. 'Here, take a look at these times.'

Toye took the paper held out to him, and perused it carefully.

FRIDAY AUGUST 20th
PM
7.40 King leaves dining room.
8.00 Wendy Shaw takes phone call.
8.40 King arrives in hall with Fortnight Film.

'If this chap King's the killer, he must have done the job

pretty smart to get back by 8.40,' he commented.

'Exactly. But even on foot, he could have been up at the bungalow by five to eight, and that's started me thinking. I've got a nasty feeling that if my aunt hadn't rung just when she did, Wendy might still be alive.'

Toye stared at him. Then sudden illumination came into his face, and he gave a brief whistle.

'Meaning the call brought her out of the lounge where she was watching the telly, and she heard somebody, and went to have a look?'

'Just that. Did you notice that the phone was in a sort of recess in the hall?...I only hope Aunt Is won't tumble to it, if I turn out to be right. She will, of course.'

They sat on in a silence which became oppressive. Toye, looking like a meditative owl behind his hornrims, laboured painfully with an idea. At last it came out.

'Seeing that Wendy Shaw was a reliable type,' he said slowly, 'it mightn't have been that she heard anything. As she was halfway there after taking the call, she might have thought she'd just go along and have a look at the kid.'

An involuntary movement by Pollard sent a paper knife skimming across the floor into a corner.

'Leave the damn thing!' he shouted, as Toye made to get up and retrieve it. 'My God, what a fool I've been! Of course King was after the kid!'

13

Here will I smell my remnant out...
George Herbert. The Temple.

A statement from the County Planning Officer was handed to Pollard when he called in at the Stoneham police station early the next morning, before starting for Kittitoe. In it, Mr Thornhurst confirmed that he had dined with Mr Donald Glover at the Crown Hotel, Winnage, on the evening of August 20 last, and that they had parted company at about 9.40 pm.

Pollard read the statement with the surface layer of his attention, while aware of the startling suddenness with which a new insight into a case transported you into a totally different context. Don Glover had become irrelevant at the drop of a hat. The stage, until so recently well occupied by suspects, now held three figures only: Eddy Horner's infant grandson, Wendy Shaw and Paul King, all three remorselessly pinned down in a circle of a spotlight.

'Thanks, Sergeant,' he said, surfacing and putting the typewritten sheet into his briefcase. 'One more for the file. Tell Superintendent Crookshank that we've gone down to Kittitoe again, will you? We'll be looking in here again later but how much later I can't say yet.'

He hurried out to the waiting car, firmly reminding himself that between moral certainty and proof a great gulf was fixed.

On the Winnage road Toye asked him if there was anything particular that he hoped to get out of Geoff Boothby,

152

their first objective of the day.

'The short answer to that's no,' Pollard replied. 'But when he hears we've nothing on him, he may be quite chatty from sheer relief—people often are. It's possible we might pick up something useful.'

'Well, one thing,' Toye said, 'Mrs Townsend was definite that the Friday night runs up to Stoneham to collect her husband were discussed on August 6, when the Horner staff were up at Uncharted Seas. So far, it's all so circumstantial, though.'

'Fair enough, but you don't often get an eyewitness of a murder, do you?'

They drove in silence for a couple of miles. The morning was cloudless, pale blue and slightly crisp, and the road almost empty at this early hour.

'King had opportunity all right,' Pollard said suddenly. 'Can we establish that he engineered it by some fiddle over the return time of the coaches, which gave him a convincing reason for fading out at the vital time? As soon as we're through with Boothby, we'll go straight to Biddle Bay. There'll be staff on duty at the company's office on a Bank Holiday.'

'What about the Fortnight Film?' Toye asked.

'We've got to get hold of it somehow, without putting King on his guard. I've been thinking about this editing business, and remembering that they've been holding these Fortnights in the area for some years, based on the Horner pub at Biddle Bay that's out of commission. Suppose King used the Winnage section of a previous year's film, cut out any shots of people, and put in sections of this year's that included Mrs Makepeace and some 1971 Fortnighters. That would have cut down the work he had to do on the Friday evening. Or he may have done it during Thursday night, of course—he must have had a key to that door near the labs. If there's been any hanky-panky with the film, I'm hoping the Forensic chaps will be able to spot it, by tests on the adhesive tape, or something.'

'How are you planning to get hold of the film, sir?'

'The only thing I can think of is to do it through Horner. He could reasonably ask to see it, or something of that sort.'

'Means telling him quite a bit, doesn't it?'

'He's bound to realize that we think the whole business is involved with the Fortnight, but after all, there were eighty members of the public, and only five Horner staff. It's a risk we've got to take, I think.'

'Wonder how he'll react to the idea of attempted kidnapping of his grandson? Remember how he dashed off to tackle Mr Glover when he thought he might be involved in the murder?'

'Yes, I do. He'll need handling, especially if things hot up.'

The suburbs of Winnage were drowsing in a prolongation of the Sabbath calm, the streets deserted except for an occasional milk float, or a family car being loaded up for a day out. The centre of the town with its closed shops was a city of the dead. Toye turned into the car park of the police station, and within a few minutes they were being received by Superintendent Bostock.

'Young Boothby's here,' he told them. 'Made no bones about coming along—said he'd rather that than have coppers round at his people's place. From the look of him, he thinks you've come with the warrant in your pocket.'

'Nothing like that, Super,' Pollard told him. 'He's completely cleared.'

Superintendent Bostock expressed relief and warm satisfaction.

'That's a real bit of good news,' he said. 'They're a decent public-spirited family, and it would have been a terrible thing for them. And there's never been anything against the lad, either...Things moving, I take it?'

'Just beginning, we hope.'

Geoff Boothby, very white and tense, was sitting slumped at a battered table in a waiting room, and gave them a quick look as they were shown in. Pollard was cheerfully matter-of-fact.

'Good morning, Mr Boothby. Thank you for coming along here : I suggested it because I thought you'd probably prefer it to our calling at the house. I'm afraid the last few days have been pretty unpleasant for you, but in a murder investi-

154

gation these things just can't be helped. You'll be glad to know that as a result of information received, we no longer have the least interest in you.'

The young man made an unsuccessful effort to speak.

'Have you had any breakfast?' Pollard asked practically. 'No? I thought not. Toye, see if you can rustle up something, will you?'

Geoff Boothby took out a rather grubby handkerchief and wiped his clammy face.

'Sorry,' he mumbled. 'I'm not the stuff heroes are made of. I've been scared stiff. Nightmares, and waking up sweating like a pig. Everything seemed so hopelessly against me.'

'You'd have been a most abnormal type if you hadn't been rattled,' Pollard replied, taking out his cigarette case. 'Fag? How sensible of you not to smoke. You've got another week's holiday, haven't you?'

'Yes, I have, thank the Lord. I feel I want to get right away. Take the car, and simply drive and drive...'

The return of Toye, followed shortly by a constable with tea and sandwiches, created a welcome diversion. With a hot drink and some food inside him, Geoff Boothby began to relax. Pollard had no difficulty in steering the conversation towards the Horner Discovery Fortnights.

'This one was my third,' Geoff said, in answer to a question, 'and it's bloody well going to be my last, I can tell you. I never want to see Kittitoe again.'

'Have the rest of this year's staff been on the job long?' Pollard asked casually.

'Mike Jay has, right from the start. That's about ten years, when old Horner first thought up the idea. Mike's really worked it out for him. Susan Crump came in early on. The Kings were recruited when I was.'

'The Fortnights certainly seem to have caught on.'

'Old Horner's mad keen on them,' Geoff Boothby replied. 'Salves his conscience, I always think, for having made such a packet out of ordinary holidays. The Fortnights barely pay their way, but people without much cash get a decent couple of weeks away, and new interests into the bargain. At least, most of 'em do.'

'I suppose Mr Horner's particularly interested in the local one, as he lives in the district?'

'This is it. He's crazy about this part of the world, and that bungalow of his. He designed it himself on the fantastic site he managed to buy, and just can't stop showing it off. He always asks the Fortnight staff to drinks the night before the show starts, and every year we're toted around the place to admire the latest improvements, and expected to say how super everything is. This year all the women had to go and goggle at the kid.'

'He's selling Uncharted Seas, you know,' Pollard remarked.

Geoff Boothby gaped at him, then suddenly looked rather shamefaced.

'Because of—of what's happened?'

'Yes.'

'Good Lord—somehow I never thought of him minding all that much. About Wendy, I mean.'

'In fact, he minds one hell of a lot, Mr Boothby.'

'I didn't mean to knock the old chap...he's a decent bloke. Not like some of the stinking rich crowd. I mean, he liked his bungalow because it was in a fab spot, and good design and whatever, not just because he owned it, and it had cost the earth. Oh, hell, I can't explain.'

'I know exactly what you mean,' Pollard said, 'and you're dead right, too. Well, Inspector Toye and I must be getting along.'

A quarter of an hour later they were on the now familiar Winnage-Biddle Bay road.

'I didn't expect to get anything as definite as that,' Pollard remarked. 'I'd been wondering what chances the Kings had had of going over the ground beforehand. We now know that Mrs King had been taken along to Penny Townsend's bedroom, and actually seen where the child's cot was.'

Toye agreed that they'd had a real bit of luck.

'You know,' he went on, 'You wouldn't think a chap could possibly have been in the bedroom, strangled a girl, got her body out of the house, and collected her handbag without leaving a trace of some sort, would you?'

'I've been thinking along that line myself,' Pollard said.

'I've come to the conclusion that we'd have found traces all right if we'd been in at the start. I'm not blaming Pike in the least. He was geared to the idea of Wendy having gone off with a boy friend, as the two Townsends were. He checked for signs of a break-in, and was assured that nothing had been disturbed or was missing. When Penny Townsend got to her room, her whole attention would have been on the baby. Can't you imagine her bashing around the place, blowing her top, seeing about the bottle it hadn't had, and so on? She just wouldn't have noticed any small signs of a struggle, like a ruckled mat, for instance. It's not as though the contents of drawers or cupboards had been disturbed. Then the next morning that damn-all daily of theirs went through the whole bungalow like a hurricane.'

'Not much hope of our finding anything now,' Toye commented gloomily.

'I'll give you that. But there might have been something Penny Townsend did notice, but which went clean out of her head in the schemozzle over the baby. If so, it's just possible that we might be able to get at it by asking the right sort of questions. We can have a bash, anyway.'

They drove straight through Kittitoe without calling on Constable Pike, past the turning to Hugh Stubbs' impeccable house and the King William, and out on to the Biddle Bay road, finally reaching the holiday resort itself. The beach and the seafront were crowded, and Toye edged the car along with difficulty.

'There's the place,' Pollard said. 'Wright's Coach Tours. Double yellow lines, though. Look, there's a turn-in at the side of the office. It must lead to a yard of some sort. Let's try it, for a start.'

Ignoring a notice saying STRICTLY PRIVATE, Toye negotiated the narrow entry, and they arrived in a small enclosed space in which several cars were already parked. He had just eased into the only remaining vacant space when a door burst open, and an elderly man charged towards them shaking his fist, and demanding in lurid terms what they thought they were doing on private property.

In reply, Pollard held out his credentials.

'We are CID officers, investigating the murder of Wendy Shaw at Kittitoe on August 20,' he said, 'and urgently require to talk to someone in authority here. Are you the proprietor of the firm?'

'Yes, I am,' replied the man. 'James Wright. How was I to know you were police, seeing you're in plain clothes?'

'You couldn't possibly have known,' Pollard replied soothingly, getting out of the car. 'If we're in the way here, I expect Inspector Toye can find somewhere else to park.'

'You're not in the way. Plenty of room for people on lawful business. It's the general public you've got to watch out for. Nobody'd believe the cheek and sauce of 'em, once they get on four wheels. Come this way, if you please.'

Mr Wright shot these staccato utterances over his shoulder as he led Pollard and Toye into the building from which he had erupted, and down a passage to his office.

'Seats there.' He indicated a couple of chairs drawn up in front of his desk, at which he installed himself, hands resting palms downwards on its top, and his bright eyes under bushy eyebrows fixed on his visitors.

'I understand,' Pollard began, 'that this firm provided coaches for expeditions from St Julitta's School during the Horner Discovery Fortnight that was recently held there?'

'Correct.'

'I further understand that on the afternoon of Friday, August 20, there was some misunderstanding about the time of departure from Starbury Bay on the return journey?'

Mr Wright raised a hand and brought it down on his desk with a resounding smack.

'Then, with respect, sir, you've been misinformed. There was no misunderstanding whatever. We had our instructions, and we carried them out. To the letter. As always. Wright's Right On The Dot. Our Slogan, sir.'

With a wave of his hand he indicated the phrase in bold red lettering, framed and hanging on the wall, and added that it appeared on every item of the firm's stationery.

'Excellent,' Pollard replied gravely. 'I'm sure you live up to it. How were the coaches ordered for these Horner expeditions? All together in advance, or from day to day, so to speak?'

'Why, you couldn't run a business like ours on a day-to-day basis, not in the season, you couldn't,' Mr Wright told him. 'It's all we can do to meet the demand with planning well ahead. Now, I've been dealing with Mr Jay over these Discovery Fortnights ever since they started up at the Horner Hotel here, the one that was burnt back in the spring. He's careful and methodical. Writes in good time, gives all the information, and asks for a quote. We quote fair and reasonable terms, and ninety-nine times out of a hundred he'll write back accepting for the lot. That's how it was this time, and everything went like clockwork till the last trip, the one to Starbury Bay on August 20. The two drivers—absolutely dependable men—came back in a real taking.'

Pollard managed to stem the torrent of Mr Wright's indignation by asking to see the correspondence. A folder was handed to him, in which he found the various items in perfect order. Michael Jay's initial letter had been written in early May. The Wright quotation had followed promptly, and the terms accepted, clinching the inclusive deal. A fourth document was a typed list of the expeditions, each with its date, times and allotted driver. Clipped to this was a memorandum of a telephone call, which Pollard read with heightened interest.

IMPORTANT
HORNER'S HOLIDAYS
Phone message from Mr Jay, St Julitta's School, received 9.15 am 19 August 1972.

Coaches to return from Starbury Bay at 3.45 pm instead of 2.30 pm, please. Charge up extra time to Horner account.
S.E.B.

'There you are!' exclaimed Mr Wright triumphantly. 'Rings to make an alteration, and then turns on us when it starts raining after dinner.'

'Who took this call?' Pollard asked.

'Mrs Banks, in the outer office. Perfectly reliable—'

'Is she around, by any chance?'

'Sure she is. This Bank Holiday's one of our busiest days.'

Mr Wright pressed the bell push on his desk, and told the youth who answered it to ask Mrs Banks to step in for a moment.

A small brisk woman with auburn-tinted hair promptly appeared.

'These two gentlemen are from Scotland Yard, dear,' her employer began. 'They are making enquiries—'

'Just a moment, Mr Wright,' Pollard cut in firmly, 'We're checking up on this phone call, Mrs Banks. Did you take it yourself?'

Looking puzzled, she took the paper from him.

'That's right,' she said at once. 'I remember it quite well. Those are my initials—Shirley Eileen Banks. It's all in order.'

'I'm sure it is,' Pollard replied. 'Did you speak to Mr Jay himself?'

'The gentleman said he was Mr Jay, of Horner's Holidays, speaking from St Julitta's School.' A defensive note sounded in Mrs Banks's voice.

'Had you ever spoken to Mr Jay before?'

She stared at him, and he could see it dawning on her that something serious was afoot.

'I believe he did ring in once a year or two back,' she said, 'But I didn't remember what his voice was like in the very least, if that's what you mean.'

'So you can't say whether the voice which gave this message was his or not?'

'No, I couldn't possibly,' she said. 'I just took it for granted.'

'Would you recognize the voice again, do you think?'

Mrs Banks thought deeply, with furrowed brow.

'I suppose I might,' she said doubtfully. 'I wouldn't like to have to swear to anything, though. There wasn't anything special about it—not an accent you'd notice, I mean. And there's always a good bit of noise in the front office, with people in and out, and the traffic. I do seem to remember that the caller sounded as though he was in a hurry.'

'Was he calling from a box?'

She thought again.

'I don't think so, but there again, I couldn't be sure. The phone's going all the time.'

Pollard thanked her for her help, and let her go. He asked if either or both of the drivers on the Starbury Bay expedition were available.

'One of 'em is,' Mr Wright replied. 'He's due to take out a trip at two pm. I'll send round for him. He only lives a couple of streets away.'

As they waited, Pollard learnt at some length that the driver in question, Will Hannaway, was an employee of long standing, and exceptionally reliable, even on the Wright standard.

When he appeared, he struck Pollard as a sensible man in his late fifties or early sixties who was clearly under a sense of grievance. It transpired that the expedition to Starbury Bay was the standard one for the last day of the Discovery Fortnight, and that he had taken parties there for several years. The practice was to spend three or four hours there, and with Mr Wright's knowledge and consent, Will Hannaway's brother-in-law who farmed in the area collected both drivers, and took them along to share the family's midday meal, driving them back to Starbury in good time for the return home.

'Hold on a minute,' Pollard interrupted. 'Did the Horner staff know about this arrangement?'

Mr Jay certainly did, Will Hannaway told him, and Mr and Mrs King had chaffed him in the coach going out, saying they'd rather have a farmhouse lunch than a picnic on the beach.

'Trouble was, sir, my brother-in-law's name not being the same as mine, they didn't know where to ring. Not that it would've have made much difference, because of the accident.'

With some difficulty Pollard got the facts straightened out. By two o'clock the weather was looking so threatening that Hannaway had insisted on breaking up the family party, and starting for Starbury, in case Mr Jay wanted to leave at the original time after all. Unfortunately, his brother-in-law's Land Rover had collided with another car in a narrow lane.

161

The driver of this car had been slightly hurt, and as the accident had happened on an unfrequented minor road, it took some time to get help, and transport to Starbury for the two drivers. They did not, in fact, get back to their coaches until just on 3.30 pm. They were greeted by a furious Michael Jay, who accused them of being an hour late. He had refused to look at their schedule, and announced that Mr Wright would be hearing from him.

'Never 'ad such a thing 'appen to me before,' the outraged Will Hannaway concluded. 'We were on time: down in black an' white, it was.'

Pollard sat thinking for some moments.

'Wasn't anything said about the time for starting back when you arrived in the morning, and people were getting out?'

'No, it wasn't. Mr Jay, he always just checks up, but he didn't travel in one of the coaches this time. Came in a young chap's car. They'd got there ahead of us, an' gone to the beach caff. Mr King, he didn't say nothin', and seein' I'd got me schedule, it didn't matter, like.'

'How long do you allow for the Kittitoe-Starbury Bay run?'

'Normal time's 'our an' a 'alf.'

'You took a good bit over that coming back.'

'The weather'd come in real dirty. There was mist over the moor, and it wasn't no manner o' good to try makin' up time, 'owever late we was.'

'My drivers acted in a right and proper way all through,' Mr Wright asserted. 'The two coaches were locked and left in a public carpark, and ran to schedule, as per instructions, as you can see from the file. As to who gave the instructions, it's not my business.'

'No one's blaming you or your drivers for what happened,' Pollard assured him. 'I must ask you to let me have that file and its contents for the moment, though. I'll give you a receipt, and everything will be returned to you in due course.'

The file was reluctantly handed over, and after warning Will Hannaway that he might be required to give evidence in court at some future date, Pollard brought the interview to an end.

Over a hurried meal Toye remarked that King had left the phone call to Wright's surprisingly late.

'I don't suppose he knew for certain until the evening before that Jay was going to Starbury by car. He may have wangled it, by offering to go by coach himself. If Jay had been on board it's a virtual cert that he'd have spoken to Hannaway about the return time.'

'But the hold-up over getting the film editing finished was vital to King's whole scheme,' Toye objected.

'So vital that he must have had several alternatives to fall back on. If the coach plan had turned out unworkable—as it nearly did, because of the weather—he would probably have given it out that the tape stuff for piecing the film together was faulty, and he'd got to go in to Winnage and get some more. Something on those lines, anyway.'

Pollard suddenly pushed his plate away, his portion of plum tart unfinished. Toye was tactfully silent, and went on eating unobtrusively.

'What's so riling about this bloody case,' Pollard went on, after a pause, 'is getting all this evidence, and yet not being able to pin anything on King. Take that phone call, for instance. There was a call box outside the kitchens at the school for general use, and desk phones in Mrs Makepeace's and Medlicott's offices. Possibly elsewhere. What price asking about ninety people if anyone saw King coming away from any of these places at about 9.15 am on the morning of August 20?'

Toye wisely made no attempt to belittle this daunting prospect, and shortly afterwards they took to the road once more, and drove in a depressed silence to Uncharted Seas. This time they were admitted by Mrs Barrow, hatted and coated in sober black, and apparently on the point of departure, having washed up the lunch things.

'This way, please,' she said. 'I'll tell Mr Horner you're here. They're on the terrace.'

She led them to the sitting room, and vanished through the French windows.

A spectacle case went flying across the crazy paving, and

there were sounds of someone struggling up out of a low chair. Eddy Horner, obviously roused from post-prandial slumber, came in and blinked at them.

'Sorry to disturb you, Mr Horner,' Pollard said, 'but there have been some developments, and I think you may be able to help us.'

Eddy Horner surfaced abruptly.

'Siddown, won't you?' he said.

'First of all,' Pollard told him, 'I want to ask you an important question. Have you had any threatening letters or telephone calls lately?'

'Not for a couple of years, at least. Nothing really serious, even then.'

'And there haven't been any threats,' Pollard went on, slowly and deliberately 'that an attempt would be made to kidnap your grandson?'

There was a frozen silence during which he watched the pupils of the little man's blue eyes narrow to vanishing point. Eddy Horner sat absolutely immobile, gripping the arms of his chair.

'So that was it?' he mouthed, almost inaudibly.

'I think so,' Pollard told him, 'and also that Wendy's murder was incidental. She probably surprised the kidnapper in the act.'

He allowed a further pause to develop so that these two monstrous ideas could be fully assimilated.

'We have a considerable body of circumstantial evidence,' he went on, 'but nothing conclusive enough to justify an arrest at the present moment. As I said just now, we need help from you at this stage.'

'D'you imagine I'd hold back?'

'No, but you will have to take a good deal on trust, and realize that I can't answer any questions. Not easy for any-one of your standing.'

'Get on with it, for God's sake, and don't waste any more time talking. What do you want me to do?'

'In the first place to help with what is bound to be an unsuspecting interview with your daughter. I think she may have valuable information which she doesn't realize she possesses.'

164

'Penny may fly off the handle, but she's always all right on the night.'

In the event, Penny Townsend's immediate reaction to the idea of an attempt having been made to kidnap her son was to stifle a scream with a hand to her mouth. She dashed out on to the terrace again, and began to drag the pram in which he was sleeping into the sitting room. Toye went to her assistance.

'Now then,' her father said, when this operation had been completed, 'the kid can't come to much harm with a body-guard of four of us. Go ahead with your questions, Super. Keep at it as long as you like.'

'It's just the same old ground again, I'm afraid,' Pollard told them.

He stated his conviction that traces of some kind must have been left by Wendy's murderer, but overlooked in the confusion of the return from Stoneham. Father and daughter sat listening with a kind of agonized intentness, a curious heightened physical resemblance seeming to manifest itself as an expression of their shared distress. Presently, at Pollard's suggestion, they all moved to Penny's bedroom, where she put the still sleeping baby into the carry-cot which stood on a low table by her bed.

After outlining what he believed to have taken place in the room shortly after 8 pm on the evening of August 20, Pollard began to question her minutely about any disarrange-ments of bedclothes, furniture or miscellaneous objects.

'For instance,' he said, 'you didn't find one shoe of a pair you'd left on the floor lying some distance from the other, as though someone had tripped over it?'

By now on the brink of tears, Penny shook her head.

'I just can't remember noticing anything,' she said tremu-lously.

'Some people have a very keen sense of smell. They can tell if a person has recently been in a room when they enter it, especially if the windows are shut, as I'm sure they must have been that night because of the weather.'

She swallowed.

'I know what you mean. I'm like that myself. But when I was changing to go up to Stoneham, I knocked over a bottle of perfume, and the room just reeked of it for ages.'

Suppressing a surge of despair at the fruitlessness of his questioning, Pollard took a long look round the elegantly furnished bedroom, ending with a survey of the carry-cot. King must have been standing beside it, surely, when Wendy came in…It was decidedly lush—in a different class from the pair acquired for Andrew and Rose. Was it remotely possible that a hair or a thread had caught on the outside?

'Mrs Townsend,' he said 'I should like our forensic experts to have a look at that carry-cot. Can you manage without it for a few days?'

'Why, of course. I could turn one of my suitcases into a bed for him.'

'If that little padded quilt was over him, I'll have that too, please.'

'It wasn't this quilt, actually. I noticed a mark on it, and gave him a clean one.'

Incomprehensibly, Pollard felt a sharp tingle of excitement go through him.

'Has the one you took off been washed?'

'No, it hasn't. It's been quite a job coping with everything singlehanded.'

On learning that the quilt was in the soiled linen bin in the bathroom, Eddy Horner went out. A few moments later he returned with a blue plastic cylinder, and proceeded to empty its contents on to the floor. Penny sorted through the crumpled heap, and extracted another tiny quilt like the first.

'This is it,' she said. 'I'll find a bag to put it in.'

Pollard took it from her and shook it out, holding his breath. There was a small discolouration on it, rather than an actual stain. He sniffed at it, and rolled the quilt up again tightly.

'Thank you,' he said, 'that will be fine. I wonder if you could spare a big plastic bag which would take the whole cot? Inspector Toye will help you pack it up.'

He caught Eddy Horner's eye, and the two of them returned to the sitting room.'

'A small quantity of the dope meant for the little chap got spilt,' he said. 'I now hand over this line of enquiry to my

166

forensic colleagues, and take up another. I want to see the last part of the Fortnight Film, which was shot in Winnage on August 18, but it's absolutely vital that you get hold of it for me in a way that is perfectly natural, and arouses no comment whatever. Can you do this?'

Completely rigid, Eddy Horner stood staring up at him without speaking.

'Yes,' he said briefly, after a long interval.

14

...those damned dots...
Lord Randolph Churchill

Sergeant Boyce was explaining enthusiastically that the photographs had been magnified two hundred times.

Pollard stared at a landscape. Who would have imagined that the smoothness of terylene masked such diversity? The quilting formed a ravine, from which a precipice rose to an undulating plain with a host of minor topographical irregularities. A blue flower of convolvulus type dominated the scene by its vastness. The central area of faint discolouration was a huge lake, fretting at its shores. And there was a deep hole suggesting the mouth of a cave, with a savage fissure radiating from it.

He roused himself to attend to the experts from the forensic laboratory, and ask some intelligent questions.

'The chap must have been startled, and accidentally dropped the syringe just as he was going to give the kid a shot,' one of them was saying. 'The jolt as it landed on the quilt, or the involuntary pressure of his thumb would account for the spill.'

'Then when he picked the thing up, the tip of the needle caught in the stuff, I suppose, and tore it?' Pollard asked, pointing to the mouth of the cave with the point of a pencil.

'This is it.'

'What was the stuff?'

'Paraldehyde. Because the quilt had been screwed up, the stink was still unmistakable before we got going on tests.'

'Where do people—lay people, I mean—get paraldehyde from?'

The expert shrugged his shoulders.

'Manufacturing pharmaceutical chemist? Dispensary of big hospital? Of course you'd have to know the safe dose to give a baby of that age.'

This conversation was the main event of Tuesday morning. Thereafter, there was nothing to do but wait for the information being gathered about Paul and Janice King, and for Eddy Horner's return to London with information about when the Fortnight Film would be available. Michael Jay, Susan Crump and the Kings would have left Crowncliff by now, and be heading Londonwards. Pollard had a mental picture of the blue Hillman, the battered estate car and the green dormobile borne along in a rising tide of traffic, advancing in a series of sweeps and checks like the sea on Kittitoe beach.

'That dormobile,' he said aloud to Toye. 'We mustn't lose sight of the fact that the original plan was kidnapping, not murder. The Kings must have made preparations for hiding the baby. If everything had gone according to plan, a terrific hue and cry would have started up as soon as the Horner-Townsend lot got home late on the Friday night. Unless, of course, there had already been a phone call to Wendy, warning against calling in the police, and stating the ransom terms.'

'Or a note made up out of newspaper type for her to find,' Toye suggested. 'All the same, the Kings couldn't absolutely bank on there not being a search. As we know they were both in the school building from 9.40 to about 11.0, the idea must have been to stow the kid away in the dormobile, safely doped to keep it quiet.'

He eyed Pollard speculatively, but drew no response beyond a resigned remark about getting down the overflowing In tray.

It was mid-afternoon before Sergeant Longman materialized with the eagerly awaited preliminary report on the Kings. He had often worked with Pollard before, and possessed an exceptional flair for nosing out the right kind of information about the past lives and present circumstances of suspected persons.

'It's all in my mind, as the doctors keep telling you these days,' he said. 'Will you have the gist of it, sir, or wait till I've got it all down on paper?'

'Have either of the Kings got a record?'

'Not as far as I can trace at the moment. No dabs yet.'

'Then go ahead right now. Never mind about their past histories.'

'They're chronically broke,' Longman began, going straight to the root of the matter...

The Kings' landlady had told him what a struggle it was to get the rent out of them, and that a chap from some moneylending concern had called to see Mr King several times lately. Discreet enquiries had revealed debts to local tradesmen in Mowstead, the outer suburb where they lived. There were no children, and they both had jobs, but splashed the lolly around when the pay packets came in, and Mr King was said to frequent the dogs. He worked full time with Horner's Holidays, often taking parties abroad.

'That may explain the shortage of money,' Pollard remarked. 'He mixes with people with more cash than he has, and both of them try to keep up with the Joneses. Is she full time with Horner's, too?'

'No, she only works for them during the summer. She goes back to her old job in the winter—the one she had before she married him, six years ago. She's a qualified dispenser.'

'What?' Pollard shouted. 'Say that again!'

Longman expanded the statement. Janice King worked in the dispensary of the South Metropolitan Hospital, which was glad of additional qualified staff during the busy winter months.

'Have I brought home the bacon, sir?' he asked.

'The whole hog, from the look of it. Listen, and I'll put you in the picture.'

He had just finished doing so when the expected telephone call from Eddy Horner came through, who had now arrived back in London.

'Horner here,' came the now familiar voice. 'The goods

will be delivered to you during tomorrow morning. I didn't consider an earlier delivery practicable.'

'Thanks very much,' Pollard replied. 'Where do I contact you after delivery?'

'The office, if before five. I've got a private line for personal calls. Otherwise at my flat here. I'm in the book. All right?'

'Fine.'

The line went dead.

'Cold steel, that little guy,' Pollard remarked, as he put down the receiver. 'In a highly emotive situation like this, he can forget he's the boss of Horner's Holidays, do what he's asked, use his judgement, and ask no questions. Single-minded to a degree I find a bit disconcerting...What sort of a joint do the Kings live in, Longman?'

'They've got a so-called flat in a ropey old Victorian house, Number Twenty, Dunsland Road, Mowstead. The lease of the whole place runs out in a couple of years, and the speculators can't wait to get the demolition gangs in. The old girl who lives there is cashing in for all she's worth, by letting bits out while the going's good. Furnished flats, she calls them, but I reckon she's sailing pretty near the wind, and that's why she doesn't try to evict the Kings, although they're such bad payers. I went along as a prospective tenant, who'd heard that someone was moving out, and got all the gen about the Kings without even trying.'

'Are there garages for the tenants?'

'No. I made a point of asking that. Their cars have to stand out. There's what was a small lawn affair in front—it was a good class house once.'

Pollard did not miss the fleeting glance exchanged between Longman and Toye. He sat doodling on his blotter, his mind moving rapidly. How he detested this stage of a case, when there was nothing to do but hang around. Or was there? A money motive behind the attempted kidnapping could obviously be established now, but what else was there to justify an arrest? No proof that King had rung the coach office to alter the time of return from Starbury, nor that he had not been fully occupied in editing film during the critical period on the evening of August 20—not so far, anyway. It's thin, he

171

told himself. Bloody thin. Suppose they did have a bash at looking inside the dormobile, as Toye and Longman were obviously raring to do? How did the chance of discovering preparations for hiding the Townsend baby weigh against the risk of alerting someone in the house, and perhaps having to make a premature arrest, with the case against King incomplete? On the other hand, mightn't any telltale evidence in the dormobile be removed during the next day or two? All told, there was ample justification for a search warrant, wasn't there?

The silence was eventually broken rather tentatively by Toye.

'It's a Roamhome B Type,' he ventured. 'I could easily put my hand on a plan of one.'

Pollard grinned suddenly.

'All right. Go and get it, blast you!'

Longman grabbed a sheet of paper, and began sketching rapidly.

'It's like this,' he said. 'Here's the front of the house, with about a forty foot depth of lawn here. Low stone wall with the railings gone on the road side, here. The wall's been broken down by the gate, so that cars can drive straight in. There's some tatty shrubs giving a bit of cover from the road.'

Pollard contemplated the rough plan.

'A lot would depend on whether the dormobile's parked just inside the wall, or bang up next to the house.'

'The local chaps could check up on that for us, sir.'

'Us?'

'Something to be said for including Our Man Who's Been There in the party, don't you think, sir?'

'You and Toye seem to be getting the bit between your teeth,' Pollard remarked, picking up the telephone receiver. 'Of course, anything to do with a car goes straight to his head...Get me the HQ of the Mowstead area, will you?'

He waited, conscious of having burnt his boats.

In the event, the operation mounted at 02.00 hours on the following morning was quite substantial. Pollard, Toye, Longman and Boyce drove down from the Yard to Mowstead police headquarters, arriving simultaneously with a patrol car, whose occupants reported all quiet at 20 Dunsland Road, and the Roamhome parked the second vehicle in, between two others.

A map was produced, and it was decided to approach the house from the upper end of Dunsland Road, which, Pollard learnt, sloped gently downhill. The patrols had noted several gaps among the cars parked along the kerb at the top. The Yard party would proceed to the spot on foot, Boyce being equipped with camera and flash bulbs. Behind them the Mowstead police car would coast down in neutral, and draw up outside Number Twenty, keeping in touch with their station by radio.

'If you're spotted, and a 999 call comes in here, we pick it up, and come forward, and say we're on a job, and not to worry if they see or hear anything. How's that?' Inspector Hallett asked.

'Fine,' Pollard replied. 'I don't see what better cover we could have. Well, I suppose we may as well get cracking.'

Ten minutes later the four Yard men were walking quietly down a deserted suburban road. There was no moonlight, but the clouds were patchy, and visibility surprisingly good. The air was chilly, but still stuffy: the pre-dawn freshness was yet to come. A light breeze rustled some dry leaves in the gutter, the sound almost indistinguishable from the hiss of tyres on tarmac as the Mowstead police car glided past, and came to rest twenty-five yards ahead. They came up to it, and passing through the gap in the wall of Number Twenty, approached the Roamhome with infinite caution.

As expected, it was locked. Toye got to work with an assortment of keys. The delay, actually only a couple of minutes, seemed an eternity, during which Pollard had ample time to visualize the complete and humiliating failure of the expedition. There was a faint click. Toye opened the door of the Roamhome, holding it until it rested against the side of the vehicle, revealing the shadowy interior. Then, by previous arrangement, he stepped inside, and Pollard mounted the steps.

He halted by the passenger seat to allow his eyes to become acclimatized. Even before this happened he sensed instinctively that the floor space in the rear was not clear. Very tentatively he switched on a small torch, pointing it downwards. To his dismay he saw an untidy heap of boxes, folders and various unidentifiable objects, and something large and shrouded which suggested a film projector. How in hell, he wondered, were they to get at the double seats along the sides, which pulled out to form the bed, and under which were the storage compartments forming the most likely hiding places for a small baby? They'd have to risk shifting some of the junk. Reluctantly, he reversed down the steps again, and broke the news to the others in a low tone.

'If anyone can get at those bunkers, you can,' he mouthed into Toye's ear. 'At any rate, you've had some experience of a contraption like this. But no risks—that's final. I'd rather pack it in.'

Toye vanished into the Roamhome.

An interminable wait ensued. Faint sounds and occasional glimmers of light came intermittently from the interior. Pollard realized that he was painfully taut, and tried to relax. He shuffled his feet, trod on a twig which snapped with a sound like a pistol shot, and swore picturesquely under his breath. Then silence descended for another aeon.

Close at hand an earsplitting yell suddenly rent the night from top to bottom, and was immediately taken up and surpassed in volume by another. The two rose to an ever heightened pitch, fell, interwove on a still rising note, and were merged in a chorus of eerie screams. Pollard held his breath. To his horror a lighted rectangle sprang out of the blank bulk of the house. Toye instantly switched off his torch. There was a wild scuffle past the Roamhome, and a low moaning started up. The lighted window was thrown open, and a swish of falling water resulted in a stampede at ground level. There was a pause. At last the window was slammed down again, and a few moments later the light went out.

Pollard expelled a huge pent-up breath. Longman performed a realistic pantomime of neck-wringing, and Boyce's shoulders were eloquent. There was an interval during which Toye's activities seemed to be suspended. Finally the faint sounds of movement and the occasional gleams of light began again.

The wait was so long that it began to seem quite impossible that anything could ever happen. Then Toye was coming down the steps.

'Got it,' he breathed. 'I'll tell you where to plant your feet.'

Pollard edged in behind him towards the double seat on the off side. Its upholstered base had been raised. Toye directed his torch into the storage space underneath. It was empty, except for folded blankets, and half a dozen tins of baby food. The ray of the torch shifted to the side of the bunker, and Pollard saw that two holes had been cut for ventilation.

'Not part of the original outfit,' Toye murmured, 'but nobody'd think anything of it, as they were keeping stores there. On the floor, on my right...'

Pollard found himself looking down at a curiously familiar collection of objects : tinned meat, fruit and vegetables, packets of tea and sugar, and other groceries, all neatly packed together, but apparently in nothing. He bent down, and discovered that they were in a transparent tray of some plastic material, about four inches deep.

'Fits the top of the compartment like a glove,' Toye said very quietly. 'Foxed me at first. It wasn't till I stuck my finger through one of those holes and found a space that I tumbled to it.'

'I'll send Boyce in. Make him keep down the number of flashes.'

There were three. Pollard stood anxiously watching the house, but there was no sign of life. Six feet of Boyce came down the steps in reverse. From inside the Roamhome came the sounds of Toye restoring the status quo. Then he, too, emerged, closing and relocking the door. As the Yard party appeared on the pavement, there came the sound of a brake being released, and the Mowstead support began to coast downhill, gathering momentum as it went.

'One of your finest hours, my old and bold,' Pollard remarked to Toye when they were safely embarked. 'Let's hope they won't notice their gear has been shifted, that's all.'

'Not them,' replied Toye with mingled gratification and disapproval. 'Using the inside of a nice little job like that Roamhome as a junk heap.'

Sergeant Boyce had the photographs ready and blown up by the time Pollard arrived at the Yard after a few hours' sleep at home.

'Good show,' he remarked, studying one of the virtually invisible tray packed with groceries. 'Of course, a chap used to a fiddling job like editing films would be nippy with his hands. He could have easily put this affair together out of some sort of cellophane material. And there was plenty of room for the kid underneath,' he added, inspecting the shot of the interior of the storage compartment, 'and air, too, for short periods.'

'You don't think it would have been discovered if the Roamhome had been searched?' Toye asked.

'It depends on how and when it was searched—if at all. We can assume a ransom demand, backed up with the usual threats. I can see Penny Townsend absolutely refusing to have the police brought in before they'd got the baby back, can't you? I think—'

He broke off as the Fortnight Film was brought in, and deposited on his desk.

Thereafter the centre of operations shifted to the forensic laboratory, where it was made clear to Pollard that his presence was not desired. He returned reluctantly to his room, and made a pretence of catching up on other cases. Before going to lunch he rang the laboratory, only to be sworn at by the expert investigating the film. It was not until mid-afternoon that he was invited to come along.

'Quite interesting,' the expert grudgingly admitted, after a routine protest about being expected to carry out rush jobs with scientific accuracy. 'Except for the last 150 feet—a usual length for a ciné film—the film is homogeneous, and has been very recently edited. We've done various tests on the transparent adhesive tape used in the splicing. The greater part of the last 150 feet was edited some time ago, and there are curious features. Sections have recently been cut out, and others inserted, which seem identical with the earlier part of the film, as far as the splicing tape goes. These insertions —there are three of them—seem to be primarily shots of people. Like a run-through of this last part? Boyce seems to be hovering.'

'I can't wait,' Pollard replied.

The projector whirred, and a length of film was run through at speed. Then the confused imagery on the screen resolved itself into a caption, which stated that the historic town of Winnage summarized 2000 years of human occupation.

Trying not to be distracted by the excellence of the photography, Pollard watched with painful concentration in the hope of detecting discrepancies. There simply must be some, he thought, if most of this film was taken last year. Or even two years ago. Of course King would have chosen one with much the same sort of weather as this year...

A cheerful group came across a medieval bridge. These would be 1971 Fortnighters, of course.

'That's one of the recent insertions,' the expert remarked, echoing his thoughts.

The film moved on to buildings: a narrow little street of small houses with built-out porch rooms, some fascinating seventeenth-century almshouses, grouped round a courtyard. A really impressive terrace of Georgian houses, and finally a Victorian monstrosity of baronial gothic type, which Michael Jay was hilariously pointing out to an appreciative group. Presumably the second insertion...

Suddenly Marcia Makepeace filled the screen, gazing up at the spire of the parish church. Shots of new municipal buildings followed, modern and functional, in carefully landscaped grounds. Now they were in the market square, crowded with shoppers and drifting holidaymakers. The camera moved on, now focusing on a stall displaying a bewildering range of garments, now on another heaped with vegetables and fruit.

'Hold it!' Pollard shouted.

'As it turns out,' Eddy Horner said, 'I'm having the usual meeting with Jay, King and Susan Crump at eleven tomorrow, to discuss this year's Fortnights, and future plans. You're saying that you want the Winnage part of the Kittitoe film run through as a natural outcome of the discussion, and to have it stated definitely that it was actually shot this season. And you're asking to be in on all this, but not visible?'

'That sums it up perfectly,' Pollard replied. 'Is it feasible?'

Eddy in dark suit, collar and tie, behind the imposing desk of his room at Horner House seemed remote, he thought, but not through boss-consciouness...

'Perfectly feasible. The small committee rooms are wired for projection. I'd better show you one.'

When this had been done, the inevitable question came.

'I take it that you may be making an arrest tomorrow?'

'It's certainly a possibility,' Pollard answered.

There was a moment's silence.

'I won't keep you,' Eddy Horner said. 'The lifts are at the end of this corridor. Can you make your own way out?'

An entirely convincing discussion was in progress in the adjoining room. Pollard listened with frank admiration for Eddy Horner's stagemanagership. He had a clear view of the meeting, through the crack at the hinges of the door of a small secretarial office leading off the committee room. The door was ajar, and he looked straight across at the white screen. Michael Jay sat on Eddy's right, taking minutes, and Susan Crump on his left. Paul King was on Susan's left.

An informal but businesslike exchange of views was concerned mainly with the advantages and drawbacks of the various centres at which Fortnights had been held. The programmes followed were also reviewed.

'There'll have to be changes next season, of course,' Eddy Horner said. 'I've decided against rebuilding the Biddle Bay hotel. The site isn't big enough for satisfactory modernisation, and I'm selling it. I've been thinking a good deal about starting up at Winnage. That place has got possibilities. How about trying out a more specialized type of Fortnight there, if the deal goes through? One concentrating more on local history and architecture. That film of yours gave me the idea, King. I take it you shot it this summer? Old buildings get bulldozed a damn sight too often these days.'

'It's bang up to date, sir,' came Paul King's voice. 'I shot it on the last Thursday of the Kittitoe Fortnight.'

'Well, run it through the projector, will you? Just the Winnage bit, I mean. This is your pigeon, really, Jay.'

There was a brief pause, broken only by the whirr of the projector, as Paul King put through an earlier section of the film at speed. Watching, Pollard saw Eddy Horner studying him with fixed attention, while Michael Jay got up and went to the window to lower the blackout blind. As he returned to his seat, Winnage once more occupied the screen.

Pollard eased the door open another couple of inches. He was aware that his throat was dry, that Toye was close behind him, and that the two constables had silently departed.

He stiffened a little as at long last the grotesque Victorian mansion appeared...Marcia Makepeace, a sudden breath of fresh air...the market...the stall selling clothes...

'Hold it!' he called authoritatively, striding into the room. Reacting automatically, Paul King had stopped the film. 'What the hell!'—he began.

'Worcester Pearmains price-tagged at 1/6 a pound, Mr King?' Pollard was surprised by the irony in his voice. 'You missed out on D Day, didn't you—15 February 1971. This film wasn't shot on the last Thursday of this year's Kittitoe Fortnight, nor were you editing it between 7.50 and 8.50 on the evening of August 20. You were otherwise, and less innocently employed during that time, weren't you? I charge you with the murder of Wendy Shaw...'

Paul King kicked over the projector. Under cover of darkness he dashed for the door opening on to the corridor, where sounds of a violent struggle and smothered curses indicated that he had collided head on with the waiting constables. Simultaneously Pollard dived for the light switches, suddenly aware as he did so of a struggle going on inside the room. He went cold, his recent vague uneasiness about Eddy Horner's reactions crystallizing in a flash. As light flooded the scene, he swung round to see him pinioned by Michael Jay, while something metallic clattered on to the polished table, and skidded off it to land at his own feet. As

179

Toye shouted an order outside in the corridor, and there came the click of handcuffs, he stooped to pick up a revolver, and slipped it into his pocket.

'Take him along to the Yard,' he said briefly, as Toye appeared in the doorway. 'I'll charge him formally there.'

When the sound of footsteps died away, he silently surveyed the scene before him. A dishevelled Eddy Horner stood at the head of the table, his face set, an appalled Michael Jay beside him. Tears were running down Susan Crump's weatherbeaten cheeks. All three were staring at him in taut anticipation of further disaster.

...he was back in the mortuary at Winnage, looking down at what had once been Wendy Shaw...

'No charge will be preferred against anyone present here,' he said, and turning, walked out of the room.

Epilogue

'You two make me feel pallid and unhealthy,' Pollard remarked across a restaurant table one evening early in the New Year.

Michael and Marcia Jay had returned from a skiing honeymoon superbly suntanned, and had invited him to a celebration meal.

He guessed that it was Marcia who had wanted the date. Since the incident at Horner House on the day of Paul King's arrest he had sensed embarrassment in Michael when they met.

'We've come back fighting fit, and with all our bones intact,' Marcia said. 'Just as well, with the programme ahead. Tell him about it, Michael.'

Once again, Pollard's trained perception registered slight constraint.

'In a nutshell,' Michael said, 'Horner's have decided to try out Discovery Fortnights on the continent, and Muggins has agreed to be in charge.'

'Isn't it super?' Marcia broke in. 'Of course, he's the ideal person to get them off the ground, with his French and German, and know-how about running holidays abroad. But would you believe it, he hung back at first, making all sorts of idiotic excuses. I had to anticipate the ambitious pushing wife.'

Pollard's and Michael Jay's eyes met fleetingly.

'I'm a cautious sort of chap,' Michael said, choosing his words carefully. 'Nobody wants to be associated with a flop. But I found out in the end from Bob Townsend that Eddy had been hatching out the idea all last year, and had marked me down for the job from the start. He'd even been over to inspect some possible localities in Switzerland. He's got amazing flair for what will catch on in the trade, so when I knew all about this, I decided I'd sign on the dotted line after all.'

I get you, Pollard thought...you were afraid at first that Eddy was trying to repay a debt...something you'd never have accepted...

'That all sounds completely reassuring,' he said aloud. 'Tell me some more about the job.'

He learnt that a suitable hotel had been acquired in the Lauterbrunnen valley. The Jays, and a botanist and a geographer were shortly having a month there to map out the various courses.

'In the meantime I'm taking a gruelling crash course in German,' Marcia told him. 'Hours of being incarcerated in a language lab. Of course, I'm thrilled to bits at being in on the job, too. I'm to be the hostess. The same job as Janice King's,' she went on, deliberately introducing the topic at the back of their minds. 'Mr Pollard, what will happen to her when she comes out of prison, with no home or work? Whatever she planned to do, it's a dreadful thought.'

'It all depends on whether she wants to be rehabilitated, and also, I think, if she sticks to her husband during the years of his sentence. Some women do, you know, and in the end something is salvaged from the wreck.'

'How on earth could they ever have imagined that they'd be able to carry off that cockeyed kidnapping?' Michael Jay, solid and sensible, looked at Pollard incredulously. 'They must both be plumb crazy.'

He refilled his guest's glass.

'Thanks,' Pollard said. 'Well, you know, I'm not at all sure that they mightn't have got away with it, if poor little Wendy Shaw hadn't turned up at that particular moment. Reconstructing, Paul King would have rung her up as soon as he got back to St Julitta's, and had stowed away the baby

182

in the Roamhome. Disguising his voice as a precaution, although as far as we know, she only met him once. He would have made the ransom demand, to be passed on, and added the usual threats about what would happen if the police were brought in. How would Penny Townsend have reacted, do you think?'

'You've certainly got something there,' Michael agreed. 'I'm as certain as one can be of anything that she'd have prevailed on Eddy to produce the cash, and take no steps to trace the kidnappers until the baby had been returned.'

'Suppose Eddy had insisted in calling in the police, though?' Marcia asked.

'Even if that had been done,' Pollard replied, 'I still think the odds were slightly in favour of the Kings, at the early stages, at any rate. It takes time to mount a full scale police operation, and just picture the roads round Kittitoe from an early hour on an August Saturday morning: cars, caravans, dormobiles—the lot. The hiding place wasn't all that obvious in terms of a routine search. And add to that the fact that as Horner employees, the Kings would naturally be tumbling over backwards to help find the kid, and avert suspicion from themselves in this way.'

'I suppose, too, that the fact that they were quite reasonably spending the weekend on the road might have helped them?' Michael suggested.

'It certainly would. Having no fixed abode is a decided advantage when you want to avoid interested neighbours, and are dodging about picking up ransom money. Whether Eddy Horner would have meekly handed over a large sum of money without even having a go on his own is another matter. But in the long term, I'm pretty confident that the Kings would have given themselves away, you know.'

'You mean that they couldn't have resisted splashing the money around?' asked Marcia.

'This is it. I think this is where Paul King's lack of judgement and control which led to Wendy's murder would have come out again, and drawn the attention of the police. As soon as the baby was safely back, the hunt would have started up. Think of the publicity, and the interest. There'd have been an investigation on a vast scale, and no doubt very substantial rewards offered for information.'

Marcia shuddered.

'I can't even bear to think that I've sat at the same table as Paul King,' she said.

Michael patted her hand.

'Let's look at the case objectively,' he said. 'What was it like from the professional angle?'

'Interesting,' Pollard said, 'because of the personalities involved, and the influence they had on the course of the enquiry. Unusually emotive, from my personal point of view. Very salutary.'

'Salutary?' the Jays queried in chorus.

'Yes. It has underlined the recurring danger of accepting even the most reasonable statements made by perfectly reliable people without checking up. I mean the statement that Paul King had to spend the evening of August 20 editing the last part of the Fortnight Film because of the late return from Starbury Bay. Because it was so convincing in the general context of the Fortnight, I let it slip through. In the end, the process of elimination brought us back to it.'

'You weren't long getting back,' Marcia commented.

'No, but en route we made life very unpleasant for some innocent people, I'm afraid. Have you any news of young Boothby?'

'He came to our wedding, unrecognizably tidy.'

'It sticks out a mile that he puts us on the far side of the generation gap,' Michael said. 'He's just fixed up an exchange year in a Canadian school for the autumn, which seems a very sound move.'

'Did you have a difficult term at St Julitta's?' Pollard asked Marcia.

'Not at all, rather to my surprise. The girls were madly excited at first, and talked about nothing else, but when nobody tried to stop them visiting the cave, and standing round Sir Toby, and gooping up at Uncharted Seas, they soon got bored, and it all became old hat. I felt rather awful myself at how soon it seemed to fade out...one does forget.'

Michael's arm slipped round her shoulders. She turned her head, and Pollard saw their eyes meet.

184

'I hear from my aunt that having arrived, Mr Glover has stopped running,' he said.

Marcia laughed.

'She always puts things so neatly. It's absolutely true. Now that he's in with Horner's over the redevelopment of what was that awful caravan site, and actually living at Uncharted Seas, I think he feels life has nothing more to offer. And because he isn't bothering about impressing people, they're beginning quite to like him. I believe he's even been known to cut a governors' meeting.'

Pollard glanced at his watch, and his eyebrows shot up.

'Good lord, I'd no idea it was so late. I ought to be at the Yard. It's been a splendid evening. I do wish you the very best of luck with the Swiss Fortnights. I'll look out for the advertisements.'

'Eddy wants a new name for them,' Michael said. 'Something eye-catching. He thinks Discovery Fortnight's firmly associated in the public mind with holidays in Britain. I've got to think up something. I suppose you haven't a bright idea?'

Pollard considered.

'What about Beckon Holidays?' he suggested. 'Pleasantly enticing. Just a faint suggestion of the mysterious and the unknown. And delightfully nostalgic for you both: your first meeting place.'

'Really,' Marcia said, 'aren't our policemen wonderful?'

*If you have enjoyed this book, you might
wish to join the Walker British Mystery Society.*

*For information, please send a postcard or
letter to:*

Paperback Mystery Editor

**Walker & Company
720 Fifth Avenue
New York, NY 10019**